The Secrets They Kept

Lakishia Banister

This is a work of fiction. Names, characters, places, events, incidents, and organizations are either products of the author's imagination or used fictitiously.

Published by Lakishia Banister, Virginia

www.lakishiabanister.wix.com/personal-page

ISBN: 978-0-692-68285-2

Printed in the United States of America

For my mother, Margaret Bailey

and my children: Shykeem, Shykera and Shykayla.

Prologue
March 27, 2014
Night

Two quick pops pierced the air, entering warm, tight flesh. Bobby was hit first. The bullet traveled through his side, exiting his spine. His eyes widened for a moment as he stumbled to the ground, dazed and dying. Jason heard the first shot and inhaled deeply to yell, but his brain had not processed the situation fast enough before the gun was aimed towards him. Pop! His body stiffened. His mouth was partially opened as he tried to squeak those last few words before he dropped limply to the ground. Blood flowed in identical red streams.

They were not in that perfect dead shape; one knee bent slightly, arms a little distance from the waist. No perfect chalk lines. Jason was belly down; eyes open. One hand under his body, the other rested loosely at his waist. Bobby was lying on his side, his hand resting on the wound as if he was trying to stop the bleeding. An unanswered question set on his brown, narrowed face. He looked more asleep than Jason. If it had not been for the thick, red liquid pouring onto the pavement, reaching Jason's hair, turning it dirty red, he would have seemed peaceful. They lay, forever stopped, at the stop sign, the dead end of their lives.

The intense sound of sirens screamed over the silence that moments ago engulfed the neighborhood. Blue and red flashes drew people from their homes, glaring at the bloody scene.

"What in the world is going on?" the man asked. He lived around the corner, just off Beautiful Lane. He spoke to another man who he'd seen standing in the road.

"This is just...," He tried to search for some interesting word and forced out something familiar. "Crazy."

"Those boys didn't cause any trouble," a woman responded with flimsy lips. She hadn't replaced her dentures before coming outside. Her tongue bounced off her lips with each word.

Dorothy rushed outside and discovered her dead son. She dropped to her knees, the grittiness of the ground not registering. She crossed her arms over her chest in misery, concealing her broken heart. "Why? I want my boy back, please!" she yelled. It was like a classic line forcing its way from a movie into the real world. Heavy sobs bounced from her vocal cords, sending vibrating chills through those standing by. She curled on the ground as if an uncanny force was preventing her from straightening her spine.

Anthony tried to bring Dorothy to her feet but was unsuccessful. One large hand caressed her soft, charming face and brushed tears from her brown eyes. Bobby had her eyes.

Now, on this night, someone had taken those eyes away from her. She'd never see them again. Her tears flowed freely, one after the other. Anthony could not hold back his tears this time. He steeled himself at his father's funeral when he was a teenager. He sucked them up after his first love broke his heart. This situation was different. The pain penetrated his heart, his stoic personality vanished. Tears traveled down his smooth, grimaced face, hanging helplessly from his chin, finally dropping onto his white tee-shirt. He felt temporary embarrassment. *How am I allowing myself to lose control? Come on pull yourself together*, he encouraged himself. Dorothy stood to her feet, but slouched back to the ground again, slipping carelessly away from Anthony's arms.

"I don't understand who would do something like this to my baby," Dorothy cried. Two men in black suits, with police badges clipped at their waists, walked past the bodies, talking to each other as if the boys were invisible, asking questions, pointing to various locations at the scene. Anthony held Dorothy's hand tightly like it was confirmation to let Dorothy know he was really there.

Dorothy's hands shook violently, but she managed to wipe her puffy, red eyes. Her brown lips were salty from the tear drops that settled there. Anthony looked into Dorothy's eyes. His confusion mirrored back. He'd never seen Dorothy so distraught. He'd never fallen a part to this degree. After overcoming poverty and a troubled life in a neighborhood where crime was prevalent, he never thought this could happen to Bobby. Not here. He thought he'd pulled Bobby out of harm's way, rescuing him from the lion's den.

Oh my, Daniel and Maria have no idea. Anthony pictured them going about their business meetings or enjoying dinner while their only son was on the sidewalk, drenched in blood. He imagined them smiling and nodding at each other for approval as they sealed the deal on the property.

A short, round lady watched from her doorstep. Her hair, tucked neatly behind her ears, framed blue eyes full of surprise. Linda Norton held her index finger to her thin lips, nibbling at her cuticles. Mr. Norton noticed the biting and moved her hand slowly from her lips. They watched the bereft couple walk to their forever changed home. No smile to greet them. No son to hug. Mr. Norton analyzed the murderous scene. He adjusted his pants as if they were falling but remained in place. He touched Linda's arm. She looked in his direction, but he continued to look straight, watching Anthony and Dorothy enter their home.

Sharon lived a few houses down from Maria and Daniel. She stood on her porch. She saw Dorothy on her knees, screaming that painful cry. She wanted to run over, offer comfort, but she was afraid to leave her children's side. She had no idea what kind of person could've shot Bobby and Jason and she wasn't about to allow some crazed maniac to stumble into her yard to harm her children. Tears dripped from her face as she covered her speechless mouth with one hand. *I can't leave. I have to stay here with my children.* She mumbled.

She loved her friends, but she had to protect her own for a moment. The situation hit too close to home. She'd seen events like this unfold on the news. She'd watched parents sobbing in front of the cameras because their child was dead. She selfishly thought, *I'm glad that's not me.* It still wasn't her, just a dear friend. She folded her arms for a moment, then released them as if she didn't know what to do with her hands. She put a cold hand around her daughter's shoulder and grabbed her son's hand briefly with the other.

A woman in a blue and gray uniform walked towards Sharon. She was tall and her black hair with gold streaks was cut neatly in a bob.

"Hello, Ma'am." She spoke professionally. Her serious, but tired eyes, accessed the area where she stood.

4

"I'm Officer Whitehead." She leaned forward to shake Sharon's hand. Sharon leaned to meet the handshake. "Are you holding up okay? I know this is very frightening, especially for someone with children." Officer Whitehead nodded toward Terrell and Nicole.

"I'm just not feeling too well right now. This is just…" She paused to compose herself. She squeezed Nicole's shoulder a little tighter. "I am a good friend of their parents." She pointed at the scene as if Officer Whitehead hadn't realized what was happening. She scanned the neighborhood as if she was searching for her neighbors, wanting the full explanation of what has happened.

"I understand."

Terrell moved closer to Nicole and folded his arms across his chest. Wrinkles lumped across his forehead. His chest moved up and down rapidly. Officer Whitehead discerned his anger and protective attitude towards his mother and sister.

"Did you hear or see anything?" She had her notepad and pen ready to take notes. Her eyes were on Sharon, waiting for a response. She read the words on Sharon's shirt silently, **I've Been A Bad Girl. Where's My Bad Boy!** A yellow smiley face winked under the words. Her hair was brushed neatly into a slick ponytail and she was naturally beautiful. The porch light illuminated her face, free of make-up.

"No, I didn't. I don't know how loud a gun is supposed to be, but I can't believe I didn't hear that," she said, obviously grieved. "This is unbelievable, just horrible," she cried. She wanted to spill her anger onto the officer, but it would not come through her parched vocal cords.

"What about you two? Did you hear or see anything?" Officer Whitehead offered trusting eyes toward the teenagers, back and forth, before stopping her brown eyes on Nicole. Sharon looked at Nicole, unsure if she heard or seen anything. It never crossed her mind to ask them. She waited for the response. She looked at the officer and gave a simple reply.

"No."

Her eyes were shy and innocent; her body language, anxious. She continued to stand close to her mother, inextricably intertwining her fingers with Sharon's free hand that Terrell released moments ago. She leaned her head on Sharon's arm and stared at the ground, stomach knotted.

Officer Whitehead looked at Terrell's demeanor. His dominate posture was evidence that he was the only male figure in the house. He looked stunned, yet serious. He parted his lips to speak before they heard a loud husky voice give a command.

"Everyone back away. Back away from the scene."

"No, Ma'am. I didn't hear or see anything." Terrell responded before Officer Whitehead faced him again, asking the question.

She jotted something down, reached into her pocket and handed a business card to Sharon. "If you hear anything, please contact the police department."

TROOPER STEVE HERRING walked to Mr. and Mrs. Norton. His hair had grown out longer than he desired. He rubbed his hand over the top of his head and the long strands annoyed him. The couple sat quietly on the front steps, watching the scene unfold, wondering what Anthony and Dorothy were yelling behind closed doors. Trooper Herring presented them with a doting smile, unseen by Mr. Norton who was slouched over, face resting in his palms.

"Mr. Norton," Trooper Herring greeted with familiarity. "I'm sorry this is going on in your neighborhood." He realized he hadn't acknowledged Mrs. Norton.

"I apologize, how are you, Mrs. Norton? How are you holding up in all this mess?" Mr. Norton responded for the them both, "I guess we are doing the best we can in a situation like this."

"Well I guess that's all you can do right now." There was a short pause as both men gazed at the flashing lights. Mrs. Norton stood. Her hair uncoiled from around her ear like a snake releasing its prey.

"I know if you knew anything, you'd let us know, but I still have to follow procedure."

"We understand," Mr. Norton said as he looked at Linda.

"Everyone back away. Back away from the scene," They heard someone shout. Trooper Herring and the Norton's looked in the direction of the voice. People moved back, never quite turning their bodies, but only taking cautious steps backwards from the dead bodies as if they were going to miss something.

"Did you hear or see anything that seemed to be suspicious?" Trooper Herring continued.

"No." Mr. Norton looked at the tall, dark man motioning people to back up. He remembered him from his early days. It was Hector. He hadn't seen him in years. He remembered hearing that Hector moved back to Virginia, but he'd never seen him, until now. *Out of all nights, Hector pops back on the scene*, he thought.

"Were you all home or...?" Trooper Herring trailed off to encourage further explanation.

"Yes, we were home."

7

Trooper Herring didn't write a single note. "Just call us if you have any information, please. To tell you the truth, some young punks from the other side of the neighborhood probably did this. It's a shame. Of course, I can't go on record with that though."

Mr. Norton didn't say a word. He only gazed down the street at the iridescent lights; Mrs. Norton rubbed his shoulders.

He did it, Mama Wesley. I swear. Please don't send me back, please.

-Angel, on her last night with the Wesley's.

Angel
April 2, 2014
Morning

I stare at my features in the mirror, wondering if I look like my mother. Is her face thin and caramel-brown like mine? I trace my Idaho-shaped birthmark with a long, skinny finger. Sharp corners, straight lines, jagged edges. I want to wipe it away with a wet towel, but it won't budge. It sits here mocking me like a fourth-grade bully.

Does my mother have an awkward mark that connects her to me? A symbol of rejection. I pick up my inhaler and put it to my mouth, inhaling deeply. My lungs inflate like a balloon, then deflates. I push the top of the inhaler again, forcing a blast of air to the back of my throat.

My lips are thin and moist, my hair short and curled. I remember watching my hair drop to the floor in a brownish circle, pooling around the black leather chair in long, concentric rings.

I brush my hair, lick my lips, and then walk out of the bathroom into a dark brown, wood-paneled hall. The dust scuttles back and forth under the dim light, which flickers on and off after it buzzes. I've seen plenty of white walls, gray, even pink, but none of my previous foster homes were paneled. I sneak past Darla's bedroom and she's sprawled across the bed, her short chubby legs poke out from under the quilt like turtle legs jutting from a shell. She is alone. *Where is Dan?*

I'm supposed to stay here until I turn eighteen, which is in two weeks. I can't wait. I'm leaving today, but Darla doesn't know. Something tells me to wake her, just tell her the truth, but I ignore the feeling. The bus leaves for Northern Virginia at 9:10 a.m. and the ride will take about five hours. Bobby crosses my mind. His face stares back at me. I want to cry, but I have to stay focused.

Last year, I had become the fifth addition to Darla's home. She had set in the social worker's office staring at me like she wanted to pinch my cheeks, so in love with me. Her creepy smile unsettled me, like the creaking of an old house, threatening to fall apart at any moment.

"You are Angel's seventh foster parent," the worker half smiled. She shuffled papers around on her desk and picked up one as if she had to read my life's story to Darla. Darla shook her head in agreement and enthusiasm. I didn't understand why she was excited about being my seventh foster parent. *Did that say something about me or her?* They talked about me as if I'd disappeared into thin air, vanishing like my mother.

"I understand," she finally said. "I will do what I need to make it a positive experience for her."

"It's not easy bouncing from home to home. This child has never met her mother. It's just a shame." She shoved the papers back into a folder and pushed it to the side as if she was glad to be done with me.

"How terrible! What kind of mother would do such a thing?"

I dropped my head, played with the thread that was slipping from the hem of my shirt to pretend I wasn't listening. Thinking how horrible of a child I must've been for a mother to do this.

"She's in your care now."

Darla and my social worker shook hands. *Nice doing business with you.*

THE NEIGHBOR'S DOG barks an ugly, small, grizzly bark. I turn back to look in Darla's room. Her feet shuffle for the blanket, trying to find their way back under. A foul odor barges up my nostrils. *The trash hasn't been taken out.* I grab the trash bag that is packed to the brim and yank it out. It's 8:33. I rush outside, tripping over a doll baby and a broom. Two older women walk down the street at that fast exercise pace, their faces sagging as if lines were magically drawn to show the wrinkles. They always look with suspicious eyes, leaning into one another as if they're whispering something about me. I feel like telling them to piss off this morning, but I don't want to draw attention to myself. I don't want Darla waking early for nothing. I press my lips into a hard line, refusing to change it to an upward curl, giving a short, fake smile, still not quite speaking.

I wish I'd grabbed my bag before taking out the trash. There is a clear path I can take straight across the street, into the woods, and I can be on the highway. I've packed four shirts, four pair of panties, two pair of jeans, my toothbrush, and two books, *Invisible Man and The Bluest Eye*. Reading has become my way of escape from the things around me, although some of the readings become too real. I leave the trash at the end of the yard and run back into the house.

When I turn the corner to the kitchen, I see Darla standing near the counter. My stomach pinches and squeezes tightly like a pulled bow. Her hair is tangled, shorts rising between her thick thighs, and red blotches fill her face. "What you doing, girl?"

I hate when you call me girl.

"Just taking out the trash." I look quickly for my bag. *Good, she didn't see it.*

"I forgot to tell you that we need to meet with your social worker tomorrow morning. She just wants to make sure you are fine and..." she doesn't finish her sentence. She reaches her thick arm into the cabinet and pulls out the pancake mix.

I don't respond.

She drops the mix to the counter, white powder puffing from the side of the box like smoke. "You know if you don't go it could prevent you *and me* from getting money. I don't want that, and I know you don't either." She speaks with her back toward me as if I don't deserve her attention.

I pick up my bag and jet down the dark hall, hoping to make it to the bathroom, which seems to stretch with each step I take. A tall figure darts around the corner, blocking my entrance. My knees are weak; it feels like something heavy has dropped to the pit of my stomach, anchoring me. His eyes are sunken and thin creases extend from the corners of his eyes like spider webs. I try to avoid eye contact and my eyes go directly to his muscular, sleeve-tattooed arm. The square-headed snake coiled around a dagger grabs my attention, its hissing tongue licking his bicep, white showing in the inner part of its jawline. Cottonmouth. I remember a fact about them, they will stand their ground.

"Move out of my way, Dan." I try to push past, but he blocks me.

"Where do you think you're going?"

"None of your business." He stinks of cigarettes and beer.

"Are you eighteen, yet?" He smiles and I feel hot, thick liquid burning in my throat.

"Just move." I try to wiggle my way around him, but it seems impossible. I back up, unsure what to do.

He lunges at me. I hear the faint hum of the eggbeater twirling, stirring the pancake, eggs, and milk. I kick him between the legs, and he drops to his knees like a falling tree. I dive for the bathroom, closing and locking the door behind me. The door is unsteady, and the lock is loose. I try my best to unlock the window. It's stuck. I hear him scrambling to his feet, taking long, deep breaths to help ease the pain.

"Open the door." His voice is calm, not loud, almost at a whisper. My stomach twists again. He can come into the bathroom with one good kick. I fumble again with the bathroom window, pushing upward as hard as I can.

"Open the door."

I hit the window one good time and a burst of air seeps through the bottom of the frame. I push again and the window comes up completely. Someone yells my name, but I don't respond. I tumble out the window, landing belly down. Air rips from my lungs like a popped balloon. I force myself to stand, one hand over my belly as I make a run for it, cutting into the woods then heading for the highway. I don't look back.

I rush onto the bus, which smells of exhaust. A brown-haired boy stands in the middle of the aisle and I push past him.

"Excuse you," a female voice says irritated.

14

I ignore her.

Another girl gets on after me. She doesn't smile, face is firm and stoic. *What's her story? Is she a runaway? Where is her mother? Is she going to visit a friend?* Her hair hangs to her ears and freckles cover her nose like a connect-the-dot puzzle, scattered here and there waiting to create a shape. She looks at me briefly, walks past, and sits behind me. The door closes and I feel as though a part of my life closes too. I rest my head on the window and think about Bobby. I see his curled, white smile. I hear his high laughter. I smell his golden skin. I feel his coarse hair. He is here with me. I feel him.

The station is further behind us. There is a gulf between me and Darla's house now. I've got to get to Beautiful Lane. I look out the window and ask myself the question that I hadn't asked myself yet, *Why would something like this happen to Bobby?*

Bobby
January 3, 2014
Morning

Ringing rattled in his ears like a fire alarm. He struggled to get his eyes opened, but the light forced them into small slits. Booted footsteps hammered toward his door and a heavy hand released three rapid knocks.

"It's time to get up," Anthony shouted to Bobby. His father sounded differently this morning. His voice was usually crisp and lively, but now it sounded tired and weak.

He shifted his body to the right and his muscles tensed in his back and neck. His shoulders were stiff. Suddenly, a memory crept into his mind like a flash of lightning, but just as quickly as it came, it fizzled away like a firecracker falling back to earth. He tried to dig it up, but the thunderous knock came again at his bedroom door.

"I'm awake," he said drowsily to his father.

Bobby crouched onside the bed, gazing at the mirror in front of him. It wasn't the Bobby he'd been used to seeing, round face, bright eyes, and brown lips. His thin face, yellow eyes, and dark lips pushed away the person he used to be like a man fading in the distance of fog, you could see his silhouette, but you couldn't quite make out who he was. Bobby closed his eyes to envision the younger, more vibrant version of himself. The Bobby that used to have big dreams, the one who said he'd never do drugs, it was him who he tried to envision, but something else popped into his mind. It was another image. *Someone falling?*

The house fell silent. There were no footsteps, just the awkward hum of silence roaming from room to room like an invisible thief. Anthony had gone to work, and Dorothy had gone out of town to visit her mother for a week.

Bobby stood up, unbalanced. His knees buckled and his weight shifted to the left. Blood rushed to his head. He tottered into the bathroom, closed the door behind him, and leaned against the freshly painted white wall.

Bobby closed his eyes briefly, but that only made him feel as if he was sitting on a spinning top. He staggered toward the shower, before turning the nozzle, but left out quickly.

He wrapped a towel around himself and laid across his bed. The squeak of the ceiling fan bothered him, but the cool air made him comfortable. He tried harder to remember what happened last night, but all he could remember was being with Jason. His own life had suddenly become a fuzzy picture, smeared with a God-like hand, hard to see.

He thought about the time his father rushed into their old home with excitement.

"We're moving," Anthony had announced to Dorothy and Bobby.

Bobby was unsure what that meant. He was so young and hadn't lived anywhere else, but there.

"It's gorgeous," Anthony added.

Bobby often replayed those words in his head like a broken record. There was something crisp and delicious about them as Anthony spit them from his taste buds. Whenever Bobby imagined those words, he'd get that same jittery feeling in the pit of his stomach and he remembered the question that stung his twelve-year-old brain, *What does gorgeous look like?*

A white t-shirt hung on his bedpost. He grabbed it along with a pair of blue jeans that were folded on his dresser, pulling the shirt over his head quickly and sliding the pants on each leg carefully. His phone rang. It was hidden under the blue and white blanket bunched at the foot of his bed, warmly wrapped around an invisible body. *One missed call.* He shoved the phone in his pocket without checking the call. Anthony hadn't prepared breakfast like he'd done for the past few days since Dorothy had been gone. It wasn't that he'd gotten up too late, but there was something different about him.

Bobby fried two pieces of bacon and one egg quickly. The saltiness from the bacon made his mouth tingle. His phone vibrated. Jason's name appeared in small blocky, white letters at the top of the screen.

"What's up!"

"Yo, can you pick me up? Mom and Dad left again." His voice sounded scratchy as if he'd been screaming all night.

"Yeah. I'll be over after I eat."

"Okay, I'm about to get dressed."

Bobby looked at the clock. 7:35. "I'll be there in ten minutes."

"Bet."

Bobby hung up the phone. He closed his eyes briefly as he chewed his food and he saw another image. This time it was much clearer. Bobby and Jason were running away from someone and hid in a building. It looked like Dell Park, but he could not piece it together to make sense.

Bobby got in the car, rubbing his cold hands together and covering his head with his black hood. He took a deep breath, releasing a small cloud of fog from his mouth. He'd been doing the same thing since he was a little boy, trying to make shapes out of the steam of his breath by circling his lips, curling his tongue, or making weird faces before purposefully blowing his breath into the cold air. He looked into the rearview mirror and watched Mr. Norton jog by casually. Before backing out the driveway, he turned on the radio, but then turned the volume almost to a whisper.

BOBBY BLEW THE horn, hoping Jason was ready to go. The curtain moved to the right, followed shortly by the side door opening. He came out to the car slowly with a blue duffle bag over his shoulder. Bobby thought maybe he'd seen the bag before, but he dismissed the thought. "What's in the bag?" Bobby asked.

"What do you mean? Stop playing for real." Bobby tried to stir the thoughts about last night. The images he'd seen earlier weren't making any sense to him at all.

"What are you doing this weekend?" Bobby tried to switch the subject to give himself more time to think about the bag, but Jason didn't say anything. He sat on the passenger side quietly, gripping the bag close to his chest before he reverted to the original question, "What do you think about this right here?" Jason pointed to the bag again.

Bobby was confused. He could not recall what he'd done, or rather what they'd done. His headache increased and he felt the urge to puke. He looked at Jason and gave him a half smile. Bobby couldn't focus on the bag right now. He turned off Beautiful Lane and wondered how he was going to function in school.

Angel
April 2, 2014
Afternoon

My dream is to move out west and I imagine myself going there before falling asleep on the bus. I used to tell Bobby elaborate stories about my mother, things to make my life seem better. I was told she'd gone west after she put me up for adoption. A tall, thin woman, with brown hair and pearly white teeth comes to mind. *Mother.*

I wake to the sound of whistling breaks. We pull into a large parking lot full of people, a tableau of stories being told, anticipating their loved one's arrival. My eyes scan the parking lot: *short, chubby, blond girl, tall, thin, white male, an older married couple holding hands.* There's no one waiting for me. Other passengers are gazing out the window, seeking their relative, friend, or whoever. I look at the girl behind me and her eyes search for someone too. She looks hopeful. She waves and smiles at someone. My thoughts about her were wrong. That's what I do. I think something about someone, only to find out I was wrong.

The bus comes to a complete halt and I'm exhausted. A few people stand to their feet to reach things overhead. Unlike them, I set my bag directly between my feet. The girl behind me stands up and rushes to the door like spilled water down a hill. I keep my eyes on her, almost wishing I was her. She runs to a guy and girl who both have up signs saying, "Waiting for Lisa Wills." One of the signs is more creative than the other, butterflies, flowers and glitter painted all around Lisa's name. She runs and hugs the guy. *Maybe she was in foster care too. Maybe she's found some relatives. Her brother and sister?*

I finally get strength to stand to my feet after the few people ahead of me begin moving forward. The lady in front of me smells of something sweet.

A sneeze tries to sneak through my nostrils, tickling the hairs in my nose, but I hold my breath and twitch my nose until the feeling leaves.

As I get off the bus a thought creeps into my mind that Dan's followed me. He's somewhere near. I stand on the sidewalk alone, wondering which way to go, feeling the urge to run to nowhere, feet hitting the pavement with rapid taps.

Taxi cabs wait in the parking lot. *I have money.* All those times Darla thought I was blowing my cash on foolish activity; she had no idea I was stashing it away from her and Dan. I jog to the taxicab that looks like it's awaiting me. The guy is skinny and dark. He looks nice.

"Where to?"

"Take me to a motel that is nearest Beautiful Lane."

He doesn't say a word. He only drives away from the bus stop quickly and heads toward my destination.

THE CAB DRIVER says this is the cheapest place, so I take his word and go inside. I talk to a clerk, an older gray-headed man with tobacco stained teeth, who smells of mothballs, and tell him I only want the room for one night. I don't know if I will leave and go somewhere else tomorrow or stay another night. I just want to get to Beautiful Lane to pay my respects to Miss Dorothy and her husband. I hope she remembers who I am. I hate going through the whole guessing game. *"Do you remember me coming to your house?" "I used to play with Bobby when you guys lived closer to Newport News?"*

"Oh yes," she'd say. "Your name is…"

"It's me, Angel." Then she'd greet me with a kiss on my cheek. I don't want to deal with that. I just want them to remember me and say how good it is to see me, under not-so-good conditions.

He gives me the key and I walk at a fast pace to get to my room. Room number 212 is on the small, white jacket that seals the key. I stride upstairs, noticing the pile of trash that has been swept into the corner of a step, a potato chip bag, gum paper, mixed with grass and dirt. I wonder whose hands were holding the potato chip bag, who chewed the last piece of gum in the pack. Why were they here? I finally reach the room and shove my key in, quickly pulling it out and twisting the handle as if someone chases me into the room. The first thing I do is take out my inhaler and force two puffs of air to my lungs. I flick the light on and discover the room's somber look. It reminds me of Darla's house, paneled walls, plain blankets and shabby curtains that don't match with anything else, with one of those big TVs jutting towards the wall. I decide immediately I am not staying another night. I turn the lights back off, so I don't think of Darla.

I peek into the bathroom, thinking of movies where people think they're getting away, but the person they are running from is extremely closer than they think. It is empty and clean. A bar of soap, small tube of lotion, shampoo and conditioner are lined uniformly in the shower like marching soldiers. I wet a cloth and press the warm cotton against my face. Suddenly, I hear an odd sound. I turn off the water, hoping the noise is only my imagination. It goes away. I turn the water on again and I am sure this time the sound is real.

A faint knock is at the door. *Who in the world is that?* My hands tighten, my feet tense, afraid to move, cemented. I feel like I should run, but I have nowhere to go. I tiptoe to the window and pull back the burgundy, fruit covered curtain a tad bit. The person stands too far to the other side of the door for me to see them. *Dan.*

I hook the chain on the door and open it slowly, allowing the chain to restrain it.

"Yes," I say softly through the crack.

"You forgot something." It is the gray-headed clerk downstairs. He sticks his hand through the ajar door and puts $2.03 in my hands.

"Thanks," I say. I lean against the brown, faded door and take a deep breath. What if that was an emergency? I don't have my cell phone. I must've dropped it when I was fighting off Dan. I pick up the motel phone to make sure it has a dial tone and it does, but I have to make it through this on my own.

I stretch across the bed and think of Bobby and his friend Jason. The last time I spoke to Bobby he was with Jason and Terrell. I can remember the laughter and how Bobby described me as his best friend one minute, then his sister the next. A tear rolls down my cheek and I quickly brush it away.

24

What happened to my friend? I wonder how their parents must feel, but my own pain does not allow me to feel theirs. I fall asleep and awake in a black room. I jump up quickly to turn on the lights and lay back down in a full lit room.

Jason
January 3, 2014
Morning

Jason pushed his covers back, moving each foot purposefully so the blanket would wrinkle off him and towards the wall. He wanted to get it so bad, feel it again between his fingers. He'd thought about it all night but couldn't remember falling asleep. There it was, placed strategically under his bed. He remembered shoving it into the corner knowing his parents couldn't spot it if they came in.

A familiar pain rested in his temple. *Baboom. Baboom.* He wished last night was different, but nights like that never turn out differently.

Jason felt the pressure shift from his temple to his forehead. He rubbed the palm of his hand over it gently to relieve the pain, but it didn't work. He pulled out the bag and tossed it onto the bed. The thick taste of beer was still on his breath. His disheveled hair waved like the ocean. A knife-cutting pain ripped through his jawline with each twitch of his lips. He placed his hand under his chin and moved it to the right and left one more time, but the ache didn't budge. Then he smelled something. He couldn't remember doing it, but the stench of it made him want to do it again. Vomit was in the burger joint bag from the night before. The sick smell of old food made his stomach turn.

Baboom! The thumping gripped his face like an ugly, tight fitted mask. He sat onside the bed, leaning his head into the palms of his hands.

Suddenly, his chest felt heavy, something hot and sour formed in his throat, saliva thickened and watered under his tongue. It moved to his lips and his stomach gurgled and pulled back. His head jerked forward as if someone punched him in the gut. Jason grabbed the burger joint bag again, but it was a little too late. Vomit was on his leg, floor, and sheets. He wiped his face sloppily with the back of his hand, ripped his sheet off the bed, and cleaned up the vomit with it.

He tottered down the hall, which seemed too long on such a difficult morning. Photos of his mother and father decorated the walls. The photos reminded him of something he wanted, or something he once had. It was hard for him to tell the difference between the two. Some people took pictures and their smiles were only for the camera, but not his mother. She was genuinely happy in that photo. Jason hadn't seen her happy like that in a long time. Her hair was pushed behind her ears and Daniel's arms were snugged around her thin waist. Jason was in the lower right corner of the photo, with one arm wrapped around Maria's leg. He was so young. His face was so round. He was so innocent.

Jason peeked out the blinds briefly and saw no other activity, but the usual, Terrell and Nicole getting on the bus, and Mr. Norton jogging. His stomach tensed. He didn't want to vomit again. He stumbled into the bathroom, knocking over the lotion and soap on the sink.

He caught a glimpse of himself in the mirror and quickly turned away from it. The little boy he saw in the photo every morning was gone. Jason had dark rings around his eyes and his face, pale. The real face that was before him every morning reminded him of who he really was, not a football star, but a junkie.

Jason reached for his phone and called Bobby, but there was no answer.

He turned on the shower and stepped into the warm water immediately. Warm drops bounced off his face, chest, and arms, soothing his body. With one hand placed under the showerhead, the water smoothed its way down his nose like a stream and dangled from his lips before splattering to the tub's base. Small rivulets formed under his feet as he closed his eyes, imagining the water as blood. One bang and there the blood would be, sliding down his face, smoothing down his nose, and the hot taste of red liquid on his lips.

This is how he thought when the drugs began to wear off. Wild things slithered through his mind like little insects looking for a hiding place, *pull back this part of the brain, let us hide here.*

There was a time when he was younger when Maria and Daniel showed him love. Now, Jason was lost, and he could no longer decide if that love really existed, or if it was something that eventually faded away like a light fading into darkness. He glanced in the mirror again, this time on purpose to see if anything changed about his features. Maybe the warm water brought color back to his eyes, removing the dark rings that hung below, but the Jason he'd seen this morning continued to grimace at him.

Jason called Bobby again and this time he answered. When he opened his mouth to speak, he realized there was a sharp pain in the back of his throat.

Bobby blew the horn and Jason peeked from behind the curtain. He grabbed his baseball cap and went through the kitchen and out the side door. He forgot something though. He threw up an index finger to Bobby, asking him to wait a moment. He wanted vitality to fill his body as he rushed back to his bedroom to get the bag, but he still felt weak and tired. He quickly grabbed the duffle bag and jumped into the car, holding it closely to his chest.

Angel
April 3, 2014
Morning

It's morning already. I am greeted by a periwinkle painting perched above the television that I didn't pay much attention to previously. Inside, the area seems placid, no noise, chaos, or even uneasiness in my mind. Outside is a different story. I get up to peek out the window and notice two people arguing in the parking lot. *Husband and wife? Girlfriend and boyfriend?* I don't know, but the cops pull up within seconds of me standing to the window. I tell myself it is none of my business, close the curtain, and get into the shower. The warm water gives my skin a pleasant sting. It calms me for a moment, and I forget where I am and what has happened. Although the shower feels perfect, I only stay in for a few minutes. I dry off and flashing lights continue to swirl in an array of painted circles outside my window like a God-like artist with a paintbrush. I wonder if Darla has reported me missing. Does she even care that I am gone?

I pull a pair of white panties from my bag, along with blue jeans and a red shirt. My shirt fits tightly around my waist, but my jeans a little looser. There is a gold framed, antique mirror hanging oddly on the wall beside the bed. Its position is off-balance and strange. I can't get a good look. After looking down at myself, I feel unkempt, clothes are loose and tight in awkward areas. I glance in the mirror but turn away quickly. Idaho is placed so strategically on my cheek. I wish I'd fall in love with it, embrace the look, but for some reason I despise it. I imagine myself peeling it off ever so gently like an old sticker, or a nasty Band-Aid, residue remaining on my face, but the sound of car doors slamming pulls me away from the thought. I go to the window and the man has been put into the police car. I know what's going to happen. She will press charges for whatever: slapping, kicking, punching her, or forcing her to have sex, and then she will drop the charges. I've seen it a dozen times. Bobby and I have watched scenarios like this unfold in our old neighborhood. Hell's Corner is what he called it.

I fix the covers neatly on the bed, smoothing out the wrinkles. I want them to know how clean I am, and I am not one of those people who trash a room, then leave my mess for another to clean. The flashing lights disappear. I pick up the phone and call a cab.

THE RIDE TO Beautiful Lane takes about fifteen minutes. The place looks different from the other side of town. I sink deep in the bucolic imagery. I'd never seen such beauty. The trees are well kept. The bushes are neat and trimmed. And the saying *the grass is greener on the other side* isn't a lie. It is greener. Gorgeous two story, ranch style, modular, and large brick homes lined the street like monopoly pieces, waiting to be used for someone's dream to come true. At least that's what I used the pieces for. I stare at the red octagon, traced in a white outline at the end of the street. The word STOP in white, blocked letters. I imagine Bobby and Jason lifelessly on the ground. I shake my head to rid the image.

The taxi driver drives slowly down the street, trying to locate the address that I've given him. I remember Bobby telling me his address jokingly, saying I will come to his house one day to visit him. I wish he was here to see me.

There's a woman standing in her yard with her sweater pulled tightly around her waist, each end neatly under her arms. She watches the cab as we drive past. There's a man in the yard too, but he goes into the garage and another man jogs toward them. I turn my head, not focusing on them, but making sure I keep my eyes looking for the house.

"Here it is," The cab driver says.

My heart sinks. All the things I've played in my mind that would happen when I got here may not happen. They may not want to have visitors. They may not be happy to see me. Sweat builds around my nose and top lip.

"Are you okay?" He asks.

I pause for a moment. I am not okay, but there is nothing he can do about it. "Yes. I'm fine," I lie. I give him $12.00 and get out the car with my bag and wave him off.

The concrete driveway leads to a detached two car garage, which also has a deviated trail that leads to the front door. The second path is decorated by small rose bushes that welcomes guests before anyone else can. I admire the balcony that juts from sliding glass doors from the second floor.

I knock on the door, but there's no answer. I wait a few seconds before delivering a louder knock, and then I push the bell which I did not see at first. There are no sounds coming from the house except the jingle from the doorbell. No television. No footsteps. No chatter. A black four door car is parked in the driveway. I look around the neighborhood. The people we passed just moments are still talking in the yard and the guy who was jogging stands with them.

My attention is drawn to another house and I see a boy sitting on the steps across the street. My first thought is to sit on the step and wait for them to return, but then I imagine what kind of questions will go through their minds when they see someone waiting for them. My second thought is to go across the street and talk to the boy. My stomach tightens when I think of introducing myself to a new person. *Hi, my friend was killed, and I came to see his parents. Oh...and I'm Angel.* I walk over to him, hoping he is friendly. He stands to his feet as I approach. He is tall and handsome. His caramel skin radiates.

"Hello," I say nervously.

"Hey," he replies with a smile.

His smile is perfect. His lips outline his teeth in such a way to show the top and bottom row when he smiles.

"My name is Angel. Do you know where they are?" I point to Miss Dorothy's house. *You are so cute.* His eyes seem to look straight through me. His face is shaped perfectly, everything matching so well; his eyes, nose, and mouth.

"Angel? Bobby's friend?" His eyes widen.

"Terrell?"

"Yeah. It's me." We try to greet each other, but it becomes awkward; he leans in to hug me at the same time I extend my hand for a shake. Then he extends his hand when I pull mine away and extend my arms for a hug. *Our first game.* We finally greet with a handshake. He walks around the back of his house and I follow him. "What are you doing around here?" He picks up a basketball and bounces it a few times and stops. "Well, I guess that's a dumb question," he says.

"I came to see Bobby's parents. I haven't seen them in years. Thought I'd come by to pay my respects." He looks sad but doesn't say anything. "Do you know where they are?"

"I saw them leave about an hour ago. They're probably trying to get everything straight for the funeral, you know."

I nod my head in agreement. He dribbles the ball again, gracefully weaving it in and out of his legs like threads through a tapestry, then shooting it into the goal. He does the same thing again, but I take my eyes off him for a moment. The older man jogs again and he slows as he approaches a yellow two-story house at the end of the street.

"When are you going back home?" He decides to rephrase the question before I can answer. "How long are you staying around here?"

I don't know. I don't have a plan, but I don't want to sound careless and stupid. "I'm going back home after the funeral."

A vehicle comes down the street and I quickly peek around the side of the house. It is a white four door, round shaped car pulling into Dorothy and Anthony's driveway. A man with black slacks and a brown leather jacket gets out the car. I remember him; it's Bobby's father. The passenger door opens, and Dorothy emerges. She has on a red and white striped sun hat; the ones you'd wear while relaxing on the beach with a book in hand. Her hair hangs past the hat, reaching her shoulders.

"There they are," Terrell alerts a little too late.

"Yeah. I see them." I watch them walk into the house. From a distance, I cannot tell some tragedy hit their home. They walk normal and are dressed like regular people. I'm not sure what I expected, sagging shoulders and black clothes. They enter the house as I watch from Terrell's yard. The ball dribbles twice and then I hear a swooshing net.

"Well…aren't you going over?"

The ball bounces again, but then is silenced. It is tucked carefully under his forearm.

"Umm…yeah. I think I'll go on over. It was good to finally see you." While glad-handing in my direction, I stretch forth my hand and he returns another shake. "I'll see you around." After the words flow from my lips, I wonder if I sound flirty. He only smiles in return.

I stand on Bobby's parents' steps again. The same feeling returns as before. I push my finger into the doorbell. A short Christmas tune rings in the house. *Do they like Christmas that much.* The tune sort of makes me smile. It makes me think of the The Wesley's. The door pulls open and I hope Dorothy greets me instead of her husband.

"Hello. How can I help you?"

Bobby's father stands in front of me with curious eyes. He is tall, handsome, beard connected to sideburns. I look into his eyes and can see he's been crying.

"Hi, Mister," is all I can say before my voice becomes low and fearful. "I don't know if you remember me, but I'm Angel." My voice staccatos a little. He looks confused for a second and a shadow approach behind him. It's Dorothy. Her eyes are red, her cheeks slightly droop, and her lips are in a hard line. I begin to think this is a bad idea. Maybe I should've stayed at Darla's, but I quickly dismiss that idea when I think of Dan.

"Is that...?" Dorothy begins a question but pauses. She crosses in front of Anthony. Her hair is longer than it used to be. She almost looks the same as I remember her.

"Angel?" She finally finishes. My heart leaps. My lips curl at each corner. *Yes, she remembers me.*

"Yes. It's me." She exudes in my direction, extending her arms and pulls me in for a tight hug. She sniffles and then releases me.

"You look good, girl," she says as she eyes me up and down like I'm a long-lost grandchild, keeping her hands on my shoulders to hold me still. Anthony remains quiet, stoic.

"Well come in," she says, welcoming me like a fresh breeze. The house is immaculate. I try to avoid looking up and down the walls and peeking around corners. That can be tempting when I enter a nice house. There's a picture of Bobby in his football uniform, on one knee, clutching a football in his right hand. I stop to admire the picture and Dorothy stops walking, also admiring it. It was like she was looking at the photo for the first time.

"It still seems so unreal," she says breaking the silence.

"Have they found who did it?" The question comes without thinking.

She turns her head and moves toward the sitting area. "No, they haven't found anyone. They don't have a motive or anything." She waves her hands as if she's giving up on something, but I know she can't be giving up on Bobby's murder.

"How are Jason's parents?"

"I've spoken to them a few times since the murders. They are just as perplexed as we are. They live over there." She points to the house that's adjacent to hers. I realize it is the house where the woman and two men stood a little while ago.

She welcomes me to sit down after standing, still gazing at various pictures on the wall. Anthony stands with us but doesn't say anything to me. He gives an agreeing nod when Dorothy speaks, but that's about it. Dorothy shifts the conversation. I don't know if it's because she cares about me, or she doesn't want to talk about her dead son right now.

"So how have you been?" She asks as she pats my leg. Anthony walks into another room, leaving us alone to discuss my imperfect life.

"I've been okay," I say, hoping the answer is solid enough.

"So where do you live now?"

Fear creeps into my chest like an evil thing lurking for my soul, grasping me, but I have to fight within to make it go away. I get nervous about her contacting Darla. *What if Dan finds me?* I clear my throat. "I live with a family in Chesapeake." For some reason I don't want to lie to her. I'd have to be an awful person to lie to my dead friend's mom.

"They let you come out here alone?"

"Yes. They have relatives nearby," I say as I eat my own words from my previous thought. I guess I am an awful person. I see Anthony from my peripheral vision pacing the floor in the next room. His phone rings, but he steps outside to answer. I look out the living room window, but he is not in plain sight.

"Are you staying until the funeral?"

"Yes, but I'm not sure if I can afford the motel the rest of the week."

"Oh…I thought you were staying with relatives or something."

I have never been a good liar. I cannot keep up with the things I've said and when I've said them. It's the hardest task in the world to keep reminding yourself of a lie you've previously told so you can keep lying.

"Yeah, but I can't stay with them, so I have to stay in a motel." I feel awful again, but I think the lie is over. Dorothy looks around, eyeing her house as if she is waiting for it to give her some answer.

"We have a guest room. Would you like stay here until the funeral is over?" I am so glad she opens her home to me. I don't have to ask as I'd intended to do.

"Are you sure it will be okay with your husband?"

"Sure. He won't mind."

I wonder for a moment where he is. He hadn't come back into the house. The door slides open as soon as the question enters my mind. He looks nervous and angry at the same time. He hits a button on his phone and slides the phone into his shirt pocket.

THE NIGHT SEEMS uncanny. I never thought I'd be visiting Bobby's house without him here laughing and joking with me. I imagine his smile, radiantly, as we talk about things that happened when we were younger. I think about how he protected me. He became my big brother, in the midst of no brothers. I owe him my all. I wish I knew who killed him. I relax my head on the pillow and try to fall asleep.

Maria
April 3, 2014
Afternoon

She couldn't believe Jason was gone.

Maria stood on the porch picking her already clean, red nails with a fingernail file she recovered from Jason's room a couple weeks ago. It was something she did when she got bored, a habit she picked up from her mother. She put the file into her pocket and pulled the pink sweater tighter around her waist. The beginning of April was never warm enough for her, but there was something she usually enjoyed about it. Colorful flowers blossoming on bushes and in gardens. Butterflies waltzing through the air with quick wings and the smell of freshly cut grass. The wind brushed against her face, pushing wispy strands into her eyes.

Maria was forty-two years old, pointed nose, thin jawline, and rosebud lips. Her oval eyes made her look younger than she really was. Her hips curved outward below her small waistline. She stared at the sky, trying to glean some comfort from nature, but she could not find the peace she hoped for.

She paced into the house and there was Jason's red, white and blue sneakers saluting her and a pair of black boots with mud hugging the soles. Maria wondered where the mud had come from. Their driveway was paved, and mud didn't accumulate in their yard from the rain. She imagined Jason at some wild house party after a rainy evening, slipping in the mud and laughing himself silly.

She let out a deep sigh and moved casually through the kitchen, rubbing her hands along the smooth, cool, marbled breakfast nook, but she stopped, remembering what she'd written the night before. It was number one on her to-do-list for the morning. She had taken out sticky notes and scribbled and doodled random things to get her mind off Jason. She tossed the first paper into the trash, and then neatly wrote "to-do-list" on the second sticky note. *1) Go into Jason's room.* Her stomach pretzeled as she penned the words.

Maria sauntered down the hall toward Jason's room, his door like a time capsule reminding her of all the things she missed. The walls seemed as if they had life, wanting to get close to her, hug her in Jason's absence. *I wish Daniel was here.* The familiar photos hung on the wall above her as she crouched to the floor. Jason looked so happy, blue collared shirt hugging his small neck, boyish hair hanging loosely on his forehead. He was her baby boy.

Wiping her nose with the back of her sleeve, she rose to her feet and realized she had to muster the courage to enter that room.

She twisted the doorknob slowly and the rusty hinges squeaked. A sweet odor floated to her nose, reminding her of Jason. His bed was unmade, covers thrown wildly to the other end of the bed, creating a mysterious shape. The floorboards creaked beneath her feet, but she was used to that by now. Maria plopped down on the jumbled blanket and wept. The fresh scent she smelled moments earlier now grazed her tongue. A bottle of body wash dripped slowly onto his pillow.

Maria picked up the bottle and closed the lid. A tear rolled down her cheek, but a smile accompanied it. She placed the bottle back on the shelf and then the bedroom door squeaked again.

"Hey."

Maria let out a loud scream, grabbing her chest as she turned around.

"Whoa. I'm sorry. It's just me, Baby." Daniel touched her shoulder to calm her and kissed her cheek. "I just wanted to let you know I was back."

"You almost gave me a heart attack. I wasn't expecting you to return until later this evening." She rubbed her sweaty palms together. For some odd reason she hoped Jason was coming into his bedroom, apologizing for the stupid joke he played on everyone and saying he returned home.

"It's okay," Daniel reassured. Daniel was altogether handsome. Everything matched so well, his lips were thin, his nose slightly pointed, and his bright blue eyes and blond hair gave him the perfect look. Maria had once joked with him about being in a boy band. "You have the look," she'd said.

"The guy who was supposed to come see the house decided to wait. He said he had some important things to handle so I just came back home." Daniel shrugged his shoulders.

Maria hated that about him. Shrugs to her were an indicator of something else, but she didn't know what. He'd say things like, *I forgot the milk* and then he'd shrug, or *that important meeting was canceled at the last minute*, and then he'd shrug. It annoyed her, but she tried to pay little attention to it.

41

She picked up a blue shirt lying on the bed. She examined it. Tears fell as she pictured Jason's body filling and expanding the cotton wear. Daniel rubbed her back but didn't say anything. It finally hit her that he hadn't shed a tear all week. *Maybe it hasn't hit him yet.* His handsome face was carefree while they planned their son's funeral, acting as if there were no worries. He didn't even cry at Jason's funeral, but she assumed he was only being strong for her. When he decided to go to work Maria questioned him, but his answer was legit. "I need to keep working so I won't think about Jason so much," he forced.

"I'm going to the garage. Do you need me to get you anything?"

She only shook her head, left to right.

Whenever Daniel was home he spent long hours in the garage picking at screws and rearranging plywood that had already been rearranged, which was supposed to be used to fix the creaks in Jason's bedroom floor, but now it sat in the garage for over a year, just being shuffled around. He'd look for things that he realized he hadn't seen in months, then he'd have to clean up whatever mess he made after he looked for it. But days like that didn't happen too often.

Maria stayed in Jason's room. Her mind went back to that dreadful night that she tried to forgive herself for. Maybe if she was near things would've been different. She told Daniel the same thing. He asked, "What could you have done?" The answer was nothing. "It was some psycho that killed him. It's not your fault."

Maria peeked out Jason's bedroom window, wondering if the cops would find her son's murderer. It seemed they weren't doing enough, but Daniel told her they were doing all they could. She needed to be patient. *Shouldn't he be impatient, too?*

42

Daniel popped back into the room. "Hey, Babe. You should come outside to get some fresh air."

"You're right. I'll be out." She wiped the tears away and left Jason's room. It wasn't until she went outside that she realized she still had his blue polo shirt gripped between her fingers, a speck of blood on the hem of the shirt, calling for her attention, something she never noticed.

MARIA STARED AT Mr. Norton's hair as he jogged in her direction. It bounced up and down with each foot that landed, the wind against gravity, his hair resembling a hot air balloon caught in the wind. He slowed down, but continued in short strides, out of breath. Wrinkles creased his chin and cheeks and although thin lines encircled his eyes, Maria liked looking into them. One eye was green and the other blue. She'd never seen anything like it before. He recanted the mysterious stories his father told him about his eyes. How they were magical and all. How he had the eyes of a superhero.

"Hey there you guys." Mr. Norton stopped and leaned to touch his toes then stood erect.

"How are you, Mr. Norton?"

"I'm fine. What about you? That's the real reason I came over, to check on you guys." His hair was wet, strands sticking to the top of his forehead, and his face red. His shirt stuck to his body and perspiration appeared on the front, back, and underarms. Maria caught him gazing at the house. She remembered Jason saying he bet Mr. Norton wished he could come back.

"Not too good." Maria shook her head in pity. "This has been very difficult. Thanks for all you've done for us so far. Tell your wife thanks too." Mr. and Mrs. Norton had come over to bring refreshments. Mrs. Norton even baked her famous pineapple upside down cake for them.

Daniel came out the garage after two pieces of plywood slipped from his grip, landing on the ground. "Hello, Mr. Norton." Daniel greeted him with a firm handshake.

"That's what I like, a man who knows how to shake a hand. That's what my father taught me back in the day."

Mr. Norton would go on reminiscing sprees about his childhood and what his father taught him. Maria enjoyed the stories about his past, but after a while it got old. She felt as if she knew everything about his life. She knew how old he was when he first pumped gas. She knew what his father told him when he first went out to cut wood to keep the house warm. She knew that his father made him rise at six every morning to exercise when he turned thirteen. She was no longer in the mood for one of those stories, especially about a handshake.

"How are you holding up, Daniel?" Maria was glad he didn't stray away from the conversation.

"I'm holding up pretty good. This has been difficult." Daniel looked down at the ground and it was the closest thing Maria had seen to sadness all week.

Something caught Maria's attention for a moment. A yellow taxicab turned onto Beautiful Lane. It pulled into Dorothy's yard, but no one got out right away. Finally, Maria watched a young girl emerge from the car. She had short, curled hair, but that's all she noticed before Mr. Norton stole her attention again.

"Alright, Maria. I'll see you another time." Mr. Norton glanced around at his surroundings.

He took off in a light jog and the taxicab drove away from Beautiful Lane.

Mr. Norton
April 3, 2015
Afternoon

Their house looked the same as it did when Mr. and Mrs. Norton lived there, beautifully crafted, white ranch style home, back deck, and two-car garage attached, but the inside changed slightly, cabinet replacements and minor paint jobs. After residing there for ten years, the Norton's decided it was time to move; there were too many secrets attached to the house. Although millennial homes were birthing and emerging from the ground like landmarks in New York, there was a two story, flat top, yellow house sitting at the cul-de-sac of Beautiful Lane. It was their new home. A chimney horned from the two front ends of the house. Black shudders hugged the square eyed windows and the front lawn was trapped by a barred fence. The cemented walkway led to the mouth of the antique villa.

Mr. Norton had told Daniel and Maria bye after making sure they were fine, but he wanted something more. He needed something that belonged to him and he wanted it back. He jogged home. He could see her curled, puffy hair to the window, the one right above the kitchen sink. She smoothed the suds over her short, thick fingers as Mr. Norton came into the house. He knew she wanted answers, but he didn't have answers to give. Not yet.

Mrs. Norton was round figured. She used to be much smaller, but Mr. Norton had come to love her shape. Her skin was a golden tan, color still clawing its way to the surface from last summer's outings, she had full lips, and thick eyebrows. She stared out the window, directly down the street at Maria and Daniel's home. She obsessed over the issue almost more than him. It was annoying and frustrating to lose something that was so important, so valuable. She didn't want the secret to leak out into the community.

Mr. Norton shuffled the mail on the kitchen table like a deck of cards, looking at the name on each one and putting the first behind the entire stack, but didn't open them. He decided they were unimportant, tossing the mail to the side and tapping his fingers rhythmically against the table like galloping horses.

"Hey, Linda…"

"What did she say?" She interrupted. She didn't want to hear about anything else.

"Well you know…" He didn't get any answers, but he didn't want to tell her that. He stared at his small Black Mamba figurine placed on the table. He had them strategically placed throughout the house, although Mrs. Norton asked him to remove them. He looked back at her. "They're doing a few things around the house, so I don't think I could've gotten much information from them. She only mentioned how difficult things have been."

He wanted to keep his composure, but he could feel the tips of his finger pulsating, the adrenaline swimming through his veins, stroking to his heart. He was as tense and anxious as Linda, but he had to keep a clear head because not keeping a clear head meant bad things could happen.

"Is that all Maria said? Did she say anything about finding it?" She scowled out the window.

"She didn't mention anything. If she had, don't you think I would've told you? Even if she did find it do you think she would have mentioned it?" He stood to his feet and paced the kitchen with his hands on his head.

All the dishes were cleaned, but she kept her hands in the warm water, allowing the suds to fizz between her fingers then disappear. There were so many things she wanted to disappear just like the suds, one pop and it'd be gone.

Mr. Norton sat to the table with his hands interlocking one another. Mrs. Norton, on the other hand, was watching something. Her eyes remained on Maria and Daniel's home. She mentally scanned the inside of their house, knowing every turn and corner. She had been in this frame of mind since she and Mr. Norton discovered it was missing.

She grimaced. Her eyes wrinkled at the corners, her top eye lashes almost meeting with the bottom. He'd never seen her look like that before, a monster trapped inside his wife. "Something is not right," she said, "I know they have the black book."

Angel
April 5, 2014
Morning

My eyes are red. I can feel it, dry and itchy. I slept for two hours straight at the most without waking. I turned on the light after Dorothy and Anthony fell asleep because I hate the dark. I've been this way since I was a little girl. My social worker said because my mother abandoned me, I am afraid of being left alone and that's why I am afraid of the dark. She said many orphans and foster children create fictitious events that may occur in the dark because they feel unprotected without their parents. I've always wondered how she'd come to that conclusion; nevertheless, it sounded accurate. And it may explain the image I dream of, or even envision at times. I can still see him moving towards me, grabbing my arms. Maybe I did make it up like Mama Wesley said.

I stand on the porch and the sun pains my eyes. I cover them with the sunshades I have in my bag. They belong to Darla. I took them two weeks ago. She never noticed.

"Are you ready?" Dorothy is dressed in all black and looks oddly fantastic, but I don't tell her though. I assume that no one wants to hear how lovely they look on the day of their son's funeral.

"Yes," I say looking past her.

She invites me into the limousine with her, Anthony, and some relatives I haven't met until the moment I step inside the limo.

"This is Angel," Dorothy says quickly.

They all say hello. Their eyes searching me, their hellos unsure.

"I am…was a good friend of Bobby's." My voice trails off into nowhere.

They nod, but never say anything. I sit quietly as they chat about small things. *Whose house are you going to afterwards? Did anyone hear from Aunt Sarah?*

We arrive at the church which I wasn't accustomed to. I just want to pay my respects, then leave. I move slowly inside the church, purposefully allowing everyone else to go in before me. I prefer to sit in the back, eyes covered, crying to myself. Mellifluous sounds come from the front of the church. Her voice is clear and deep. Everyone around me smells of mint, candy being pushed around, clicking, and crunching against their teeth. The church is a mid-size building. The entire structure, inside and out, is not fancy. The burgundy carpet stretches all the way from the entrance to the place where the preacher stands. Behind the preacher is a huge picture, an image of Jesus Christ in a white robe, his arms extended to the people sitting in the congregation. It is supposed to make a person feel warm or welcomed I guess, but it gives me a different effect. It makes me nervous to know that I am always being watched by a greater being. I don't have any privacy.

The funeral begins and Dorothy's sobs are heard at the back of the church. I know if I look at her it is going to make me breakdown in tears. The preacher talks about Bobby's personality. I wonder if he really knew him.

He speaks for twenty minutes, ending the message with kind words to the family and leaves the pulpit to shake the hands of everyone who sits on the front row. He gets to Dorothy, leans over, and kisses her gently on the cheek.

We leave for the burial site. Anthony keeps his arms around Dorothy's shoulders as they are the first ones to walk out the church behind their son's casket. I imagine Bobby's stiff body rocking back and forth with each step from the six men who carry him.

Anthony peeks over his shoulder, causing me to do the same when I see him. It's a natural habit. I've got to see what someone is looking at to understand facial expressions, or what caused them to turn around in the first place. He looks over the other shoulder too, scanning the area. I turn each time he does, but I don't see anything or anyone who is trying to get his attention. He does it three more times, looking behind him and on each side as if he is waiting for someone to approach him.

The family sits in front of a pearl white coffin, trimmed in gold. I think of my friend lying in there, stiff-like, eyes closed, arms folded across his chest. I wish he knew I was here with him. It is my first time coming to a burial site. I'd been to a funeral before, but not for someone who was close to me. There was a friend of The Wesley's who had died, and they thought it was appropriate for the whole family to pay respects even if we didn't know her personally. I had sat in the church gazing at the ceiling, thinking *I wish I can leave now.* We went straight home after the preacher's message. Everyone was still happy.

After the preacher monologues, each person on the first row stands to their feet, a rose in hand. They toss the rose on the casket. Dorothy tosses hers. Anthony tosses his. An aunt, uncle and grandparents toss theirs. More words are spoken before the casket is lowered into the ground. Heavy sobs mixed with metal cranking. *Hell's Corner.* I turn away again and saunter closer to the parked vehicles. Others trek away too, slow and painful, greeting and hugging each other, rubbing backs and kissing cheeks. Anthony gazes around as he'd done previously. And for a split second we make eye contact. With all the people who are casually walking by, or standing still to talk, we are at perfect angles where there is no one blocking our view from one another. I quickly take my eyes off him, hoping there's a possibility he didn't see me staring.

TERRELL IS OUTSIDE. I change into a pink shirt with a gray jacket over it. I rush past Anthony who stands close to his bedroom door, but never going in. I give him a head nod but keep downstairs and out the front door.

"Were you at the funeral today?"

"Yeah. I saw you," he says.

I want to switch the subject.

"Are you an only child?"

"Nope. I have a sister. Her name is Nicole. She's with Mom right now."

He is so handsome. His facial features are nothing like mine. It all comes together so well. It is without blemish. He looks at me and I see his eyes shift to "the mark" then to my eyes. I rub my fingers over it.

"How'd you get that scar?" He blabs it out like it's a part of a normal conversation. Shouldn't questions like that be under the rude category?

"It's a birthmark."

He gazes down the street as a car pulls onto Beautiful Lane.

"Do you talk to them at all?" I ask. The car turns into Jason's driveway.

I watch Jason's dad get out the vehicle. All I can see is the back of his head before he enters the house.

"Do you talk to them?" I ask again.

"Not much. My mom and I have gone over to say we're sorry about what happened. My mom talks to them all the time. She's just a caring person like that."

"It must be hard for you too." I didn't mean to go there again with him, but it is the obvious conversation right now. It is always on my mind, lingering in the background like a song replaying subconsciously, waiting for me to blab it out at any moment. I don't have answers and really no one does, but I want them.

"Do you know what happened that night? You weren't around?"

"We were cool, but I didn't hang out with them like that." He paused and licked his lips. I admired the action. "They did things I didn't do."

"What do you mean by that? Bobby was a good person," I say, believing my own words.

He looks confused but doesn't refute it right away. "I've known Bobby for a long time, and he was there for me." The words come out with a sting as I envision Bobby protecting me. I wanted to say more, but more wouldn't come out. We stand quietly as the sun is being pulled down behind the trees like a cordless window shade.

"I get that. I'm just saying we didn't hang out like that. We played ball together sometimes and that's about it. That day you talked to me and Jason for the first time, we all just happened to be on the basketball court together."

"So, what kind of things did they do that you weren't involved in?"

Terrell looks away from me, trying to avoid the question. I don't take my eyes off him. I touch his arm, pleading him.

"What are you talking about? Please tell me. He was my friend. I cared about him." I can tell he is giving in. He shakes his head as if he is about to betray someone by giving me this information.

"Alright, alright. Bobby and Jason were both into drugs. They hung out at Dell Park all the time and that's where the drug users and drug dealers hang too. The police have talked to a couple of people, so I heard, but haven't found any real information." He rubs his hands across his face as if he can't believe he just told me this.

"Will you go there with me?" The question comes out fast and naturally.

"Go where?" He looks at me as if I've lost my mind.

"To the park. Maybe someone knows something but is afraid to tell the cops."

"I don't know. I...I...don't know if I want to go out there and you shouldn't go either. You don't know what it's like out there." He stares in the direction of Jason's house.

54

"Look, I met Bobby in a rough neighborhood before we moved away from each other. I think I can handle this park. Okay?" I try to walk away, but he grabs my arm, only tight enough to keep me from walking away and forces me back to him.

"I get what you are saying, but I'm trying to look out for you, that's all." He loosens his grip from my arm.

How are you trying to look out for me when you don't even know me?

"Thanks, but no thanks. I owe this to Bobby." I drop my head and take a deep breath. The days in our old neighborhood cross my mind. He throws his hands up and backs away like I'm an officer putting him under arrest.

"I'm going in the house now. Good night."

I close the door behind me and there is complete silence in the house. I'm upset that he won't go with me, but I begin to understand how he must feel.

The quietness disappears when I hear a faint voice. I walk past the sunroom and there's Anthony talking on his cell phone. I stand nearby to hear what he's saying, hoping he doesn't see me. He paces back and forth, one hand waving wildly as he speaks.

"I said I will have your money."

He pauses, then says more.

"You stay away from us. Do you hear me?"

There is another pause and I try to piece together the conversation.

"I just need more time. That's it." He chuckles, but it's like a pleading chuckle.

He listens to whatever the other person says then he hangs up. I move away from the sunroom quickly and dip into the bathroom. My heart feels like it is about to bounce out of my chest and fall heavy to the floor like iron. I can't imagine what the conversation is about, but it makes me nervous. I turn the nozzle and splash warm water in my face and turn it back off, hoping it would give me some life, but it does nothing. I'm still confused by what I've heard.

He paces down the hall, then stops. His shadow stills directly in front the bathroom door. I back away slowly, holding my breath, wondering if he saw me standing by the sunroom. Maybe he knows I heard something. I turn the water on again to generate noise. I stare at the crack under the door, hoping he will continue down the hall. He stands there for another second which seems like forever, then moves past the door. His dress shoes hit the wooden floor like a small hammer. The sound vanishes slowly. The nervousness leaves, tension rolls away from my shoulders like a mud slide, taking everything else with it. I can breathe now.

Bobby
January 4, 2014
Morning

Bobby gazed at the ceiling while he rested on his back. His black sleeveless shirt- the one he cut the sleeves off two summers ago just because he felt like it- vibrated with each heartbeat. He should've been frightened, but he wasn't. Adrenaline rushed through his veins like an avalanche each time he thought about what happened. Although the pain was gone, he rubbed his forehead, remembering himself falling to the ground and hitting his head on a small object.

Jason had told him everything. He began to remember bits and pieces from that night, seeing someone being pulverized like crazy, the kicking and punching was something he'd seen before. Nothing to get nervous about. He wondered for a moment what happened to that man. He visualized the money blowing over the ground as Jason told him. Jason had looked at Bobby with excitement in his eyes as if he'd been dying to retell the story to someone. Bobby's eyes stayed on him as he gripped the bag enthusiastically. He opened it several times, revealing to Bobby what was inside.

Bobby rubbed his eyes to awake completely. The nasty taste of morning breath roamed his mouth. He stood to his feet and stretched towards the ceiling. His boxers clung to his waist like a rubber band to a wrist. The fresh scent of lemon usually filled the halls and would float under his bedroom door. Dorothy cleaned the house thoroughly every Saturday morning, but she was not there. Bobby enjoyed the fresh smell, but this morning he was glad he didn't have to meet her in the hall before going to Jason's. He'd always feel guilty about his actions the night before if he saw her the next morning, all smiles and proud of her son. Bobby put on his gray sweatpants and eased himself to the bathroom. He gazed at his reflection when he brushed his teeth, turning his cheek from side to side examining himself.

HE PUT HIS hood over his head and shoved his dry, cold hands into his pockets. He saw Mr. and Mrs. Norton walking down the street at a fast pace, their arms moving back and forth quickly with each step. Bobby waved to them. Mr. Norton smiled politely and waved too. Mrs. Norton only stared then turned her head. Bobby saw it. He assumed she was not in the mood until he saw her look at Mr. Norton, tell him something, and he glared directly at Bobby as if some deep secret was told to him. All Bobby's mind managed was *Teenage code: when you say something about someone, do not turn around to look immediately. It will be obvious you're talking about them.*

Jason met Bobby to the front door before he could ring the bell. He was dressed in a black sweatshirt and his black pajamas. He didn't look thrilled like he did the day before. The front of his hair was pushed back, and the sides were frizzled. He looked serious.

He waved Bobby into the house.

"What did you do?" Bobby stared at the hole that was now in Jason's floor.

"I had to hide the money somewhere," he said without enthusiasm.

Jason reached in the place where the wood was missing and pulled out the bag. Bobby smiled, but he noticed something else.

"Did that come with the bag?" It was only a book, but he wondered why it was hidden in the floor. *Maybe it came out of the bag.* Jason only stared at him but reached in the hole again and pulled out the little black book.

"I didn't know you write in journals," Bobby laughed as Jason handed it to him. "Is it for therapy or something?" He continued laughing. Jason wasn't.

"Read it," Jason said firmly.

Anthony
April 5, 2014
Morning

Anthony leaned over the sink to spit the white foam out his mouth and then washed his face. It seemed all too normal for him, something he did before heading to work, or playing golf. The day arrived where it was time for him to bury his son. His mind was numb like feet on a cold day. All he could envision was Bobby's narrow, brown face.

He stepped out of the master bathroom and into his brightly lit bedroom. The sun shined through the curtains, tiptoeing its way across the floor as if it was trying to find him. Anthony slid open his closet door to choose from one of the many suits he had. Each time he did this he was reminded of times when he hardly had anything. When he was a young boy his mother received hand-me-downs to give to him and his two sisters. The clothes always smelled of mothballs and had little spots here and there. Anthony removed a suit and gently placed it on the bed.

He stared at himself in the mirror, wondering how his decisions got his family into this painful situation. *Am I the cause of Bobby's death?* He couldn't live with himself if his answer to his own question was yes. Dorothy would need to know the truth, if he was the reason she was hurting so bad, but he couldn't accept it. *Whoever killed Bobby is the one who's responsible.* He buttoned his black dress shirt and slid his legs into his pleated, black pants. He looked at himself in the mirror, and unlike previously, this time he was fully dressed. He rubbed his hand down his sleeve and adjusted the collar of his black jacket.

Anthony tilted the bottle of cologne onto his finger and dabbed it on his neck. *Dabbing cologne, adjusting suit, too normal.*

Dorothy fiddled with the doorknob before coming into the room. She watched Anthony screw the top back on the bottle of cologne and place it neatly in front of the stack of sympathy cards he received from co-workers. She'd been crying and Anthony noticed. He recognized how painfully gorgeous she was. He smiled in her direction.

"Are you okay?" He asked.

"I guess," she shrugged, "What about you?"

"It's a day I hate to see." He tightened his necktie, his right hand cuffed perfectly over the knot and his left hand holding the opposite part and gave her another smile.

When it was time to get into the limousine Anthony overheard Dorothy inviting Angel to join them. He assumed Dorothy could gather information from Angel concerning Bobby's death. When she first came to the house Anthony was hopeful. He thought maybe she'd come to visit them, to tell them some hidden information about Bobby's murder, but she knew nothing. From that point on he was uninterested in her visit.

Anthony gazed at the brick church where his son's funeral would take place. He wished he could run away, rewind the tape, or make things different, but he couldn't. There was a long line of relatives and friends filing outside the church to pay respect to his son. Anthony cleared his throat and adjusted his tie as he tried to hold back the tears. The day no longer felt normal. His palms were sweaty. Beads of sweat formed around the crease of his nose. He pulled a handkerchief from his pocket, quickly wiping the perspiration and shoving the handkerchief back.

They all lined up in pairs, Dorothy and Anthony in the very front like it was a privilege to be the first in line like school aged children. Two men with funeral home emblems pinned on their jackets stood to the right of them. One had a black beard with hints of gray strands sticking out comically in various places. The other guy was much younger. He was in his mid-twenties, sophisticated, and very polite. Anthony imagined where Bobby would be when he turned 25 years old. *Businessman, grad school, NFL.* That image disintegrated, not with relief, but like a bomb detonating and blowing people to shreds.

The funeral directors allowed them to enter the sanctuary. Everyone looked at them with droopy eyes and their lips in a hard line, slowly curving downward. Anthony raised his head and saw an older woman with pink glasses. *Maybe a teacher,* he thought. He saw another woman in a green dress, *maybe Bobby's friend's parent.* He looked again and spotted Terrell. He felt sorry for him. Anthony's chest tightened as he got closer to the front row. Although the casket was closed for the moment, he could picture his son lying in the pearl white box.

Dorothy rubbed her hand in a circular motion over his back. If she hadn't, he would have yelled to the top of his lungs in a matter of seconds. He removed a handkerchief from his pocket again and wiped across his eyes.

Anthony thought the night of Bobby's death was the worst day of his life, but after being at Bobby's funeral and hearing the memories of his son, he realized this was the worst day of his life. On the night he was murdered it was still fresh, unbelievable. It was as if Bobby could walk through the door at any given time, his smile brightening the room. It didn't seem real. But today was different. He was in the coffin, embalmed, eyes closed, tight lips, and there were no hopes of him returning home. A lump formed in Anthony's throat. The lump only came when he tried to fight the tears; if he let them flow the lump would vanish. Dorothy cried on his shoulder. All other cries and voices were silenced, not because they weren't there, but because he couldn't hear them for hearing Dorothy's and his own.

As they left the church to go to the burial site, Anthony held Dorothy's hand tightly. He needed her just as much as she needed him, but he had to be strong for her. He watched Bobby's teammates carry his casket from the church to the burial site. Grackles flew above the trees, squeaking their songs to one another. Anthony watched the group of birds swoop down and then back high in a playful manner.

An ominous feeling came over him that made the hairs on the back of his neck stand. The feeling was as real as him burying his son, a bizarre feeling that someone was watching him. The back of his head tensed, and a tingling sensation moved from his shoulders to the middle of his back.

He turned to look, but he didn't see who he thought he'd see. There were only relatives and friends coming out the church.

Anthony and Dorothy walked under a big green tent with white lettering on the side, Bailey's Funeral Home. A thick green rug was laid on the ground with eight chairs facing the coffin, lined neatly over it.

Anthony and Dorothy sat in the red suede chairs. Her parents, brother, and his two sisters followed them and filled in the rest of the chairs. Each of them was handed a red rose as they took their seats. The man with the gray strands in his beard said a few words, a cousin sang a song. They stood one by one to toss their rose on top of the casket. The younger of the two men said a few words of encouragement and thanked them for believing Bailey's Funeral Home served well with preparing Bobby's body. Anthony twitched at the thank you. He didn't want to ever see the day where he'd have to allow someone to take care of his son's body. He hated the words.

It wasn't fair to Anthony that he could go on with his life, but his son's life was over. He didn't graduate high school. He didn't attend his last prom. He will never know what real love felt like. Anthony's blood line stopped with Bobby. No grandchildren, no one to carry on his life. Once Anthony was gone, *he was gone.* He tried to hold back the tears again, but the thoughts were too strong. He didn't want Dorothy to see him break. He hugged his aunt, then his co-worker and a few others, but then he was motionless, gazing at the blue sky looking for hope.

Suddenly, the same eerie feeling hit him again. He looked around, but saw no one, only Angel in clear view. She stared at Anthony for a moment then gazed into the sky. He wanted to ask if she was okay, but he walked away, still hoping the man would not show up at his son's funeral.

DOROTHY DIDN'T FEEL like all the craziness that happened after funerals: people coming over to eat, talking, laughing, their children all safe on their laps, or sitting close by their parents. She just wanted to go home to be alone, curl under a blanket. He heard the sobs as he walked towards the bedroom door, but he didn't go in.

Angel came out the guest room and Anthony stared out the window as she rushed out the house. He saw her greet Bobby outside and wondered if they knew each other before she came to Beautiful Lane.

Anthony opened Bobby's door. He pictured him standing to the mirror brushing his hair and smiling at him. He pulled the door shut and leaned against it. A tear dropped down his cheek. He wanted to see Bobby again. He wanted to be a dad again, but it was all taken away from him. Anthony walked into the bathroom and splashed water on his face. He reached for the towel, but his phone rang, startling him. *Restricted.* His heart dropped.

"Hello."

"Well, now since you've got that behind you maybe we can get to business," the voice said. Anthony still wasn't sure who *he* was, the man behind the voice.

"This isn't over. I've just buried him."

"What does that have to do with me?"

Anthony inhaled deeply, but he knew he'd have to maintain his cool. He didn't want anything crazy happening again. He tip-toed back downstairs so Dorothy wouldn't hear his conversation.

"Just listen. All I'm saying is my mind is not where it needs be right now. I have too much...," Anthony was interrupted.

"Why do you keep making this about you? You know what you owe me, and I want it, or your wife won't have either of her closest men alive."

He cringed at the thought. He couldn't imagine how Dorothy would make it without him in her life. He imagined a frail Dorothy, hurting and weeping continuously for the loss of her son and husband.

"Are you understanding what I'm saying?" The man asked. "I just want to make sure that part is clear."

"I get it. But can we discuss this another time?"

"No! I've given you enough time. Now where is it?" The man yelled.

"I said I will have your money."

"Talking it isn't enough. I need to see it, or you and Dorothy will see me."

"You stay away from us!"

"Do what you have to do to get it. Isn't that what you did the first time?"

"I just need more time. That's it." Anthony felt powerless now. What he thought was once right has turned out wrong.

"I am giving you seven days to have my money. That's it! Or I'm coming after you and your wife." The only sound remaining was the hum of a dial tone.

ANTHONY NOTICED THE bathroom light on. He couldn't remember hearing Angel come back into the house, but he knew it was her. He wanted her to go home now, or wherever she came from. He stood to the bathroom door, but he didn't hear anything. No moving. No water running. No toilet flushing. He started to knock on the door to ask if she was okay, but the water suddenly came on and he moved away from the door, thinking how he could get this man his money in seven days.

Jason
January 4, 2014
Morning

He was better than he was yesterday, especially after what he and Bobby found a couple days ago in Dell Park. There was a chill in his room that brushed against his cheek like a soft hand. He turned on the small electric heater, the spinning blades cutting through the cool air. The bag they found was pushed under his bed in the corner closest to the wall. Jason kneeled, belly on the floor and stretched his arm under the bed to reach the blue bag. It was heavy. He tugged it gently, then again with force, pulling it to himself. He opened it, revealing the cash that was inside. It looked just as enticing to him as on the day they found it. He wanted to hide it in a more secure place, but he didn't know exactly where.

His room was basic. A built-in bookshelf above his bed, which held random things, books he never read, a pair of boxing gloves, some of his hats, and some bodywash he rarely used. It was only when he wanted to get some girls that he'd douse himself in the shower with the liquid soap. His flat screen television was mounted on the wall above the cherry wood bureau and a black, leather chest was at the end of his bed.

He paced the floor and the familiar creak under his feet annoyed him, causing him to lose focus. He opened his closet door, hoping he could think of some place to stash the money, but he came up with nothing. His closet was like War of the Worlds, filled with unfolded clothes, scattered as if people were zapped from his closet and their clothes just floated to the floor. He pushed the door shut and paced the floor.

The floor creaked again. Jason yelled and stomped on the spot where it squeaked. He stomped in another area of the floor, but if felt different, a little steadier than the first. Pushing his foot into the floor again, he realized the floor was more unsteady than he'd thought.

Jason reached for the fingernail file that was on his shelf, one of the odd items that didn't quite fit the idea of what belonged in his room, but he knew it was left by his mom. He pushed it between two pieces of wood, trying to push the loosened piece from the floor. *There!* He forced his index finger under the piece of wood and balanced it so it wouldn't fall back into place. He removed it, then another, and another from his floor.

The bag would fit perfectly in the secreted spot. It was a done deal for hiding the money. Before dropping the bag, Jason removed a few hundred-dollar bills, zipped up the bag, and then dropped it in the floor. But a small, square object caught his attention. *A little black book.* He was puzzled by it. Not puzzled by the object itself, but about it being hidden in his bedroom floor. Maybe it was his dad's, but he couldn't make sense of that. He rubbed his fingers over the leathery cover, brushing the grime away. He looked at the back of the cover and rubbed his fingers over the thick dust. He saw a small emblem inserted in the right bottom corner of the book, a black mamba. He flipped through the pages, not really seeking anything, but just wanted to see if something had been written inside. And it was.

Jason opened the book.

The message inside was not addressed to anyone. There was no Dear Diary. No Hello. No Good Morning. No Dear God. It went directly into the mind of the person who was writing.

Maria
April 5, 2014
Night

She wanted to pray, but she felt it didn't work. It was the easy thing everyone told her to do, so easy, but so hard. *Just pray about it. Praying makes things better.* It didn't seem to help now. Maria searched the refrigerator for something stronger, something she assumed would help her misery right now. The guilt was eating at her. She thought if only she hadn't been in Florida with Daniel on a business trip, she would've been home with Jason. She imagined Daniel rubbing her thighs as they were by the pool while her son was being gunned down back home. A car door slammed. The urge to drink crept upon her like a lion stalking a prey, but she had to resist it now. It wasn't just the thing with Jason anymore. His murder was not the only thing eating away at her like acid annihilating flesh. It was more than that.

"Hey." His eyes looked exhausted, but his shoulders were upright. His creased gray slacks still looked good on him, his lilac shirt tucked neatly into his pants. Daniel was already loosening his necktie.

"Hey," she mumbled in return.

Maria kept saying to herself, *IwontaskIwontask.* She repeated the words in her head as if it was part of a recital, trying to persuade herself that she could do it. Daniel's facial hair was growing back. It made him look a little older, but attractive. Maria liked that about him; he could look young one minute and older and mature the next, two different people. A thick trail of cologne followed like a small child as he moved past her. He tossed his cufflinks on the breakfast nook. One of them swiveled around carelessly, making a dinging noise against the marbled nook before it finally settled. She watched him carefully. Maria knew if she asked him that one question, he'd say he was at the office, showing another house at the last minute, or the guys wanted him to come to the bar after work.

She could feel anger crawling like a spider, inching down her neck then arms. She started doing things she couldn't control. Her chest cavity moved up and down quickly. She could not get the cup to steady in her hands. Her eyes narrowed and wrinkles formed across her forehead in thick lines. She wanted Jason back. She wanted to feel and know normality between her and Daniel again.

He walked past her, and a key of anger unlocked what she was trying to keep in.

"Where have you been?" She snapped. As soon as the words rolled from her tongue, she burst into tears.

"I've just been riding and thinking. I have a lot on my mind, okay?"

He is right, she thought. Maria wanted to back off the moment he said it. They both had a lot on their minds, but there was something different about Daniel, his cologne, his clothes, and his hair. Everything just seemed different to Maria.

"Thinking about what? What could've had you out this long after work?"

Daniel faced Maria. His shirt was half undone, and he pulled his tie completely off. Even in a messy situation like this he was still handsome, sexy. She imagined him against someone else.

"Oh…you've forgotten our son was just murdered? Well let me remind you. Just last week our son was *murdered* right on this very street!" He yelled. He pointed his hand toward the street. "Do you remember now? Do you know what I've been thinking about now?"

Her heart sank as she thought about her son lying in a pool of blood. The words were unbearable, but true.

Daniel's eyes softened. His lips moved, but he had a difficult time formulating the words, mixing them to make sense. "Listen, Maria, I…"

Maria stormed past him, slamming the bedroom door.

"You are like my little sister." He throws his arm around my shoulder and smiles.

A tear falls from my face.

"Don't worry about it," he says. "I won't let anything like that happen to you again.

-Angel and Bobby, one week before she left the Wesley's

Angel
April 7, 2014
Morning

I feel a sense of purpose today, something I have never felt before, a quick surge of vitality. The question and reason for my being has always lingered in my mind. *Why am I here? What am I meant to do?* Today feels different. I am going to Dell Park so when I get out of bed today, I pay little attention to my scar and get into the shower. I wanted to go to Dell Park yesterday, but Dorothy invited me to church with her. She said it is helping her get through this hard time. I felt a little more comfortable being there than I had before.

    The warm water soothes my skin like a nerve soothing pill. I allow it to drizzle down my back and run between my thighs and down my legs. I stand still for a moment, loving the feel of the water. I think of Bobby. Jason. Darla. The Wesley's. Dorothy. Terrell. *He's so hot.* And Dan. *I hate him.* Each goes through my mind and curlicues back around to Bobby. His face is still present in my mind. I can't believe he is gone and there is nothing I can do about it. I hate that we split up and went separate ways. Tears roll down my face, but I quickly wipe them away.

Terrell's words ring in my head again and again. *Bobby was into drugs.* I can't imagine it. He hated seeing people selling and doing drugs in our old neighborhood. How could he become what he hated? He said that's why his dad moved them to Beautiful Lane. They needed a fresh start. Bobby said his dad didn't want him to get caught up in that lifestyle. I turn off the water and get out the shower, reaching for the towel at the same time. It takes me no time to get dressed. I put on a white, long sleeved shirt, although the day seems too warm for it, and a pair of jeans. I open the door and Anthony greets me in the hall. My heart leaps. My shoulders tense. He just stares at me, and then he speaks.

"Hey, Angel."

"Hi," I return.

He moves past and goes into the bedroom. It's so odd. I head for the door, not looking in the living room for Dorothy to say bye to her. I just want to get out of here and head to Dell Park before anyone can see me there.

Terrell's mom and sister stand outside, but he's nowhere in sight. Maybe he's still asleep. *What was his sister's name? Nicole?* I play it safe and give a simple wave instead of calling out names. His mother continues to stare, then waves me over.

"Hello," she says with a smile. "My name is Sharon." She shakes my hand while Nicole glares at me as if I have food plastered to the side of my face. Maybe she grimaces at my birthmark.

"My name is Angel." After I give my name, I feel like she is waiting for me to explain why I'm still in town, eyes wide, nodding head, silent, waiting for more information. I don't give her what she wants. "Is Terrell home?"

76

"Yeah. He's upstairs." She looks back at the house as if he is peeking out the window at us.

"And you must be Nicole." The name comes back to my remembrance clearly. I hold out my hand to shake hers, but she extends an unconfident hand and draws into herself. She flutters her eyes for a moment, and it causes me to do a double take. Not because it is abnormal, but I think about myself and my birthmark and then I look at her beauty, there's no scar, only a quick flutter of the eyes. Her flaw.

"She's shy," Sharon confirms.

"That's fine. I used to be the same way," I lie. *Why did I lie?* There was nothing to lie about. That is the kind of thing I hate about myself. I'd meet someone with some small problem and then I'd lie and say I deal with the same thing to make them feel comfortable. Mama Wesley recognized that character flaw in me. Every time someone had a headache, I'd miraculously get one too. If someone's eyes were burning because of the bleach when she'd wash clothes my eyes would burn too. Hit your toe, well guess what I felt that, and my toe hurts too. Despite everything, I miss Mama Wesley.

Sharon smiles at Nicole and tells me it was a pleasure to meet me. I don't know how I am such a pleasure. I easily gait down the street, not quite sure how far Dell Park is from Beautiful Lane, but Terrell said it is approximately a twenty-minute walk. I can handle that. Sharon drives past me and gently taps the horn.

I come closer to Jason's house. It looks so peaceful. Small bushes are lined up beautifully against the foundation of the house. The bushes are neatly trimmed with little purple and white pedals sticking its head from the foliage. Someone emerges from the side door. It's Maria. She looks like she's going back to work, coiffed and dressed in a black pinstriped pant suit. It must be difficult. Lose a child, bury him, and then off to work a few days later.

She waves then gets into a small, silver Volvo. I am not a fan of naming cars, but I know the name of this one. I'd seen it in a magazine when I lived with Darla and fell in love with it. I pictured myself in a red one; windows rolled down, and wind brushing against my face. The car starts and the engine revs as she presses on the accelerator. I don't look back. The car slows down then comes to a complete stop.

"Would you like a ride somewhere?"

I do, but I don't know what to tell you because I don't want anyone to know that I'm trying to find out who killed Bobby.

I hesitate.

"I don't mind," she reassures.

"Well…sure." I get into the car which smells of cinnamon. The car deodorizer hangs on the rearview mirror.

"I'm Maria. What's your name?" Her voice is mundane; dismal. I guess the voice of someone who has buried their child.

"Angel." I keep looking straight and so does she.

"Are you a relative of Dorothy's?"

Here go the questions. The same one that Sharon probably wanted me to answer without her asking.

"No. I am…was Bobby's close friend. We knew each other for years." Her face seems to drop just a little, lips forming unconsciously into an upside-down U.

"I'm Jason's mother. The one that…" she doesn't finish her sentence and I don't want her to.

"I know. Ms. Dorothy told me who you were."

She quiets. She drives a short distance before asking, "Where are you going?"

I don't want her to drop me off at Dell Park. I continue to look for something that is nearby so I can walk there.

"I don't know the name of the place, but I will know it when I see it." She buys the lie and keeps driving.

There's Dell Park. A big oval sign hangs in the center of mottled, decorative steel, designed for the sign. I look around quickly and see a pharmacy. It is attached to another store, Dave's Hardware.

"That's the place." I point to the pharmacy thinking will she believe that I didn't know the name of it. It doesn't matter. I just want to go to Dell Park to talk to someone, anyone. She pulls in front of the dingy white building and smiles. "I've got to get more." I hold up my asthma pump and shove it back into my pocket.

"Be careful walking back. It may take you about twenty minutes to return. Do you have a cell phone? Maybe Dorothy or Anthony will come out to get you."

Dang it. I forgot I need to buy a cell phone. "No. I don't have a phone, but I will be fine. Thanks." I close the door, so she doesn't make any more suggestions and she drives away. I pretend I am going into the pharmacy until I think she is clear out of sight. Someone walks behind me to go into the store, but I allow them to past me, hearing the cowbell ring above their head.

Around the corner, about a block up, I see the sign again. DELL PARK. The sign is unwelcoming, covered in dirt and rust, each letter faded a lighter shade to hide its presence from the world.

I enter through a mangled fence carefully that looks like wanton hands created shards for fun, twisted metal for comical relief. The park is empty. Only three people scrounge around, isolated. I envision the park being full of grass at one time, but dust covers most of the ground, with patches of dead grass springing up like clawed hands from underground, digging its way up for life. I imagine the park as if it was gorgeous. Maybe being a place where families once visited on warm Sunday afternoons to spend time with their children, having picnics. A guy sits on a wooden bench. He cuts his eyes at me, but when he sees me looking, he turns quickly. His hair looks greasy-thick, clunks of strands stuck together, mended by dirt and oil. I must talk to him. There is no one else closer. I imagine Bobby and Jason stretched across the hood of a car, gazing up at the stars, high as the stars.

Two older men, one with a beard and the other's face I cannot see, talk by the brick apartment complex that seems to be connected to the park. These tall buildings encompass the park, creating a dirt-like peninsula. I move closer to the guy sitting on the bench. I am afraid, but I don't show it. He sees me and frowns. His nasty teeth peeks through his parted, cracked lips. *I can't believe Bobby used to hang out here.* After seeing this place, I know there would be no other reason to hang here except to do drugs.

I sit beside the man, but not too close. My shirt vibrates, palms sweaty. He continues to look straight as if he doesn't see me. His face is covered in a thick, gray beard. I look away and remove a picture of Bobby from my pocket. I stare at the photo, trying to decide how to ask him the question. *Have you seen this kid? Do you know what happened to my friend?* I hold up the picture to the man.

"Excuse me, Sir. Have you seen my friend around here?"

He looks at me and turns his head. I look back at the picture, feeling like giving up. I stand, waiting for him to stop me from walking away. I want him to tell me to wait like people do in movies, and then give all the information I need. He doesn't do it. He only ignores me. I take two more steps and decide to try again.

"Please, Sir. I need to know if you've seen him." I hold the picture up, waiting for him to look at it while I plead with him. "My friend was killed, and I just need to know if you've seen him here." I pause. He looks at the picture. "Have you seen him here with a white kid?"

He looks closer at the picture, snatches it from my hand and stares at it. He looks as if he wants Bobby to speak through the photo. His eyebrows go closer together. His nose scrunches upward. I suspect he has seen Bobby before, but I don't want to get my hopes up. He hands the picture back to me without saying a word as if he doesn't care. *Maybe he doesn't.*

"Have you seen him before," I cooed.

"Yeah, I seen'em," he says. His voice is scratchy. Phlegm rattles in his throat like loose change.

I smile as if I have solved something, but I haven't scratched the surface yet. This could come of nothing.

"When was the last time you saw him?" I continue to hold the picture in my hand as if he doesn't know who I'm talking about anymore. Bobby smiles at us. His green collared shirt is tucked neatly in his khaki pants. It must've been game day when the photo was taken.

"He is here all duh time." He talks about Bobby as if he is still alive, like he's seen him last night. "I seen'em 'round here wit dat other fellow. Dey should stay away from here."

"Did they get into a fight with anyone around here that you know of?" I sit beside him again, moving my butt closer to the edge of the bench, turning my body towards him and leaning in a little. The acrid smell makes my stomach turn.

He scratches his head and coughs. He snorts, pulling everything from the back of his throat into his mouth like a tornado sucking in bits and pieces from the earth and hacks it out. *Disgusting.* I don't flinch.

"Dey wasn't in any trouble, but someone out here was." The way he speaks reminds me of all those times Mama Wesley made me practice enunciating my "th." *It isn't dem, duh, dey, or dat, she'd say, it's them, the, they and that. Speak with intelligence baby. People judge you by the way you speak.*

"What do you mean?" I probed.

He looks around as if there are tons of people around us. The two men who were standing beside the building are gone. The man who was wandering aimlessly is gone. No one, but me and this guy are here, which starts to scare me when I think about it.

"Dat night dem boys foun' dat money. I saw duh whole thing. I stood over dere by dat tree and watched." He pointed to a tall pine tree, the only thing that resembles life in this park. I wait for him to give me more information.

"Dat boy's daddy was out here. I don't know if dey was together or what, but dey was here duh same night."

"Wait a minute, whose daddy?" I ask. He points to the picture that I'm holding in my hand. Bobby, all smiles. I hold up the picture to be sure.

"He was out here duh same night all dat happened," he says as if I know what he is talking about.

"All what happened?" He has my full attention, I'm interested. I stand to my feet, wanting him to spit the words out as quickly as he spit the green phlegm.

"Dat boy's daddy was almost beat to def out here by three guys while his son and dat other boy stood right over dere," he pointed again, "and hid behind dem big barrels." I look over my shoulders and see two orange barrels awkwardly positioned beside the apartment complex. An old couch rested against the cans. I imagine people sitting on the couch at night, leaning back to rest their heads on the dirty barrels.·

"And what happened while they were beating him up?"

"Dose boys messed around and stumbled on dat money dat his daddy," he pointed at the picture again, "hid in dose barrels. Money was flying everywhere. Dem boys took it and ran."

I'm lost. My mind orbits around the idea of Bobby and Anthony being earthed into chaos. I can't grasp what he tells me. Why would Bobby take the money that belonged to his dad? None of this makes any sense. I turn to walk away, but I only make a complete circle, standing in the exact location I left. The man looks at the ground as if he doesn't know I'm still here.

"What happened to his dad?"

"I don't know. Duh men ran after dem boys, but nothing came of it."

"How do you know?"

"Because I saw dem boys leaving that building after duh men were gone. Duh boy's dad got outta here when duh men stopped beating him."

"How do you know it was his dad?" I ask. Maybe it wasn't Anthony after all. Maybe it was someone else and this drug using guy thinks it was Bobby's father.

He looks at me for the first time since we've started talking. His eyes are traced with dark circles and the skin under his eyes sag, two empty sockets. "I see dem two together all duh time when

83

dey come into town. You see dat sto' right dere?" He points up the street. It's the pharmacy and hardware store. "I saw dem go dere together a few weeks ago. You see dat sto' over dere?" It was a clothing store, something I didn't notice when Maria brought me in town, I would've had her take me there. It probably would've made more sense. "Dey go in dere together sometimes. I see duh dad driving duh car one day and duh son may drive it the next. I knew it was dem dat night."

"But isn't it hard to see out here at night?" I am sure there is no way he could've possibly identified them in the dark.

He pauses and turns his head away from me. He looks up and my eyes follow his. There is a row of pole lights down the center of the park. "When dose lights are on, you can see everything *if* you pay attention." I look up at the lights then around Dell Park again, a place where everything can be seen at night, but no one cares to even pay attention.

Maria
April 7, 2014
Morning

Maria still had on her nightgown. It smelled of Daniel's cologne. Although she was still mad with him, he'd manage to rub his face against the back of her gown, wrapping his hands around her waist without her noticing. She didn't discover the weight of his arm on her waist until 3a.m., then she gently moved it to the side and laid on her back.

She had dreamed of Jason last night. That's what caused her to awake. He wasn't the older Jason, but younger. She missed dreaming of him, seeing those baby blue eyes and kissing his forehead. He was on a swing, asking her to push him harder, but she wasn't near him. Jason wore plaid shorts and his blue polo shirt, which was too big. He yelled, "Momma, come push me." She was dressed in a short skirt, standing in front of Daniel, twirling her fingers in her hair, smiling at him. "Momma, come push me." She moved closer to him. The closer she got to him she noticed Daniel turned further away from her and Jason was getting older. A girl appeared beside Jason. His hair grew before her eyes. His legs no longer dangled from the swing, but the tip of his toes rubbed against the sand. The girl who sat beside Jason started to cry. Maria stopped in her tracks midway. She looked back at Daniel and he was no longer looking at her. She looked at Jason and he was rubbing the girl's arm trying to soothe her. Maria smiled, but suddenly the girl released a halting scream and Maria awoke.

THERE WAS COMPLETE silence in the house except the alarm buzzing. Daniel left the house without saying a word. She listened to the sound of tires against the asphalt as he backed out the yard. She was afraid now. Things were not going well between them and she could feel the tension building as each day progressed. She could feel him slipping away. It was like watching the sun setting over the bay; it would go down slowly and you'd hope you could catch that moment, the moment where the sun glowed so spectacular over the water, and never let it go, but then it ended. The sun was gone, and the glow had vanished. Maria wondered if things were as bad between them as she perceived.

She wanted to do something, but staying home wasn't one of them. *I'll go to work,* she thought. Yesterday she considered the possibility of returning to work to show a piece of property to a couple, but she felt guilty. Why should she return to work? But she remembered the long, drawn out days of thinking about Jason, wondering how she could've saved him, and imagining what in the world Daniel had been thinking. Today needed to be different.

The warm, sudsy water trickled down her back as the lavender shampoo thickened the water. Instead of Jason being on her mind this morning, it was Daniel. He'd seem to be wrapped around Jason, the both of them intertwining through her mind. She once thought things were getting better when they went to Florida, but when Jason was murdered, everything went back to the way they were before.

She dried herself and her hair, getting dressed in a pinstriped suit, a purple blouse, and a pair of black heels. She stepped onto the sidestep when she noticed Angel. She hadn't officially met her. Maria guessed she was a relative of Dorothy and Anthony's, but she knew that assuming things never meant she was right. Her lips curled on each side, artificially. Maria waved to Angel and she returned a brief, mechanical wave. She pulled her keys from her purse and pressed a button that made a chirping noise. She watched Angel traipse past her driveway as she put the car in reverse.

She slowed the car when she reached her, not sure exactly of what to say to her. "Would you like a ride somewhere?" Maria asked when she pulled beside Angel. Maria noticed the hesitation but reassured her. Angel said yes and got into the car. Maria finally knew her name. *Angel.* She liked it. It seemed protective.

As she drove, she finally asked where she wanted to go. Angel pointed to a pharmacy store. Maria couldn't believe she was going to walk that far. She glanced at the mark on Angel's face. She asked herself if it was a birthmark or was it something else. It didn't seem normal. Maria pulled in front of the store to let out Angel.

"Be careful walking back. It may take you about twenty minutes to return. Do you have a cell phone? Maybe Dorothy or Anthony will come out to get you."

"No. I don't have a phone, but I will be fine. Thanks."

As Maria drove away, she continued to look in her rearview mirror and noticed that Angel never quite went inside the store, she stood there, looking awkwardly at her surroundings as if she was looking for someone, or something. She disappeared from the rearview mirror as Maria drove further away.

THERE WAS ONE car in the parking lot, Crystal's. Crystal drove a small, burgundy Toyota. Maria looked around the parking lot again, but Daniel's car wasn't there. She picked at her nails nervously, wanting to bite them. That desire came shortly after Jason's murder. Just like the easy drinking.

Where is Daniel?

She walked into the office and could only see the top of Crystal's head behind the cubicle. She was on the phone and Maria was glad. She didn't want anyone to ask how she was doing. She knew she would break down as soon as she opened her mouth. Crystal looked at her and smiled, tapping a pencil against her desk. Her tan skin always looked so smooth, without blemish. Her solid black bob shifted from side to side whenever she shook her head like the person on the other end could see her. Maria waved, then walked into her personal office.

A wedding picture greeted her, a gentle reminder of their past happiness. It stared at her from a carefree world, everything so normal and still. Her face was thinner. His eyes bluer. Their soft lips connected in the photo. She wondered what people would think if they separated. Would they be seen as failures? Then it hit her. People wouldn't think otherwise about him, only her. Surely, they would think something was wrong with her, after all, she was in his shadow. She was the one who lived in a rented room downtown after finishing her undergrad in business. She was the one who couldn't land a real job for almost two years after graduation. He was the one who mentored her and gave her a chance to grow in the real estate business, putting her in a licensed program. People would think she did something wrong. How could a man so pleasant, friendly, and handsome have any flaws? She cringed at the thought and knew she had to do something to rectify the situation, whatever the situation was because she wasn't even sure.

She sat down at her desk. There were a stack of untouched papers waiting for her since she'd gone to Florida. She remembered what the plan was when she returned. Everything had to be signed and given back to Crystal to copy and file. She shoved the stack to the corner of her desk and walked to Crystal who was just hanging up the phone.

"May I have the master schedule for the showings today?" She asked Crystal. She smiled, but it faded almost immediately.

"Sure." She handed the schedule to Maria, looking in her eyes. Maria could see there was something she wanted to say. She imagined the many questions she wanted to ask flying around in her head, one waiting to land on her tongue.

"Thanks." She looked at the schedule for her and Daniel. She wanted to have lunch with him. She could not wait any longer for the perfect time. She bit the side of her lip and pushed loose strands behind her ear.

She had to show a house at eleven o'clock and that was the only one. Daniel had to show a house at 10:30, another at 11:30, but he did not have to show another house until two o'clock. Lunch time would be the opportunity to talk. She thought she should take the initiative to fix this. After all, Daniel did have to run a company and maybe she'd been too hard on him about his whereabouts. She never thought about how much pressure he may be under. She wondered if he neglected her or was she the one being neglectful. One of them had to be willing to admit fault for their marriage to get better. She needed him to help her get through Jason's death. She pulled out her phone and texted him.

Can we meet for lunch?

She anticipated the response, picking up the phone, putting it back down and making sure the volume was turned up. Then it buzzed.

Yes. Meet me at our favorite place at 12:30.

Our favorite place, Maria thought. It was Riverside Seafood and Grill, a place they'd gone numerous times for special occasions. It was the place where he'd asked her to renew their vows. It seemed like moons ago since that happened.

She arrived at the restaurant a few minutes early, but Daniel was already there. She could see him through the window taking his seat. After parking the car, she carefully applied lipstick to her lips and smacked them together.

Daniel waved to her when she entered, acknowledging where he was sitting. Maria's heels hit the floor in rhythmic beats. It was once music to Daniel's ears.

"Hello."

"How was your morning?" He asked.

"It was a little busy, but not too bad. I just had to fill out some paperwork and then I showed a property this morning." What she meant to say was she needed to fill out the paperwork, but she hadn't done it. She was too busy worried about how to make things better with him.

A waiter moved in their direction before any other questions could be asked or answered. His hair dirty blonde, his chin small, but his cheeks plump, like his belly.

"Are you ready to give your order?"

Daniel looked at Maria and gave a nod to order first.

"I'll have water and your chef salad please."

"And you, Sir?" His belly directed toward Daniel.

"I'll have a turkey club sandwich please and water as well."

Daniel unbuttoned his jacket and looked at Maria. His eyes were soft for a moment, but then turned business-like.

"So, you want to talk?" He asked.

"Yes. I do. Well we both should talk, not just me."

He shook his head in agreement.

"I just feel like things are not the same between us anymore."

He looked out the window for a split second as if he wasn't expecting the conversation to begin like this. "Nothing's wrong. I am..." His voice trailed off. "There is too much going through my head. I'm trying to act the best way I know how. I don't know what "normal" is anymore. Things are different now." He put two fingers from each hand into the air to show his quotations around the word *normal*.

Maria shrugged her shoulders, realizing she'd done something she hated about him.

"Things are different, but we don't have to change."

"Don't people change?"

"Yes, but our love shouldn't."

He knew she was right. There was something about love that he'd experienced and seen before. His mother had been sick, but his father still loved her, if not the same, deeper. He remembered how he felt when he and Maria first met and when they got married. The feeling was unshakeable, strong. It seemed as if it was going to last forever, never failing.

91

"Well yeah, but..." he had nothing to finish it. They sat quietly, gazing out the window then back and forth at each other.

"Here is your water. I will return with your food," the waiter interrupted.

There was silence between them.

Daniel took a sip of water, enough to merely wet his lips. The waiter returned and sat their food on the table. The clanking of silverware replaced their conversation. Maria hoped Daniel would continue where he left off. She stabbed the lettuce and tomato and put the fork between her lips.

He took a bite of his food too. It seemed like forever since the last word had been spoken.

"I do agree with you that people change," Maria finally said, "but I think something else is going on."

"Something else like what?" He tossed his fork back into the small salad that came with his sandwich. "Your mind is playing games with you. Please don't go there." His lips pressed into a hard line. "I don't want to deal with accusations right now," he fought back.

"I am not accusing you of anything. I am just asking for the truth."

"I have given you the truth."

Maria thought about those same words he'd given her three years ago before she discovered his infidelities. She picked through her salad with the fork, removing the onions that she forgot to ask them to remove. She looked around and the place was almost empty. She dropped the fork in her salad with force.

"You know I see you. I watch you go through your phone. I see the smiles that come on your face when you read certain messages. I know nothing from work is making you smile like that." She second guessed herself when Daniel denied everything, but once she recapped the things she had witnessed, she remembered why she suspected something was wrong.

"I can't deal with this right now. I have a ton of other things going on. Can we deal with this when we get home?"

"Are you kidding me? It isn't time for either one of us to show a listing and you are about to…"

"Crystal called before you came and asked if I could squeeze one in and I told her yes," he interrupted.

"She called you? Well cancel it then. You know you have the power to do so if you choose. And where were you this morning?" There it was, the question she knew would turn the conversation further from her original goal. "Why didn't you come in? You were awake and out the house before me." Maria had not taken another bite of food since the conversation turned tense. Her fork still held on to the onion she planned to remove.

"I don't believe this," Daniel said. "Let's finish this talk later. I'm leaving." He fumbled through his wallet and removed a twenty, dropping it on the table. He pushed his chair back, screeching it over the floor and left Maria more concerned than when she came. Her hands were folded under her chin and her eyes watered. Maria watched him drive out of the parking lot. He never looked back.

Angel
April 7, 2014
Early Afternoon

After visiting Dell Park, I find my way back to Beautiful Lane. It feels like hours since I've been gone. The guy in the park said Anthony was being attacked. *Why would someone attack him? Why would he need to give someone a ton of money?* Questions buzz through my mind like a cloud of bees and the more questions that arise, the more stung I feel. The neighborhood is quiet, like it normally is. Nicole is the only one outside. She looks my way, doesn't wave at all. I wonder has she always been like this. I think about my own story and in some odd way, force it upon her to make sense of her shyness. My story doesn't match her though. The story fits her like a too big, flimsy outfit.

I glance at her again before I walk into the house and this time she is not looking at me but staring carelessly into the sky as if she is searching for some answer that she has longed to receive. The house smells peachy. Dorothy's footsteps are thumping overhead.

Anthony isn't here. I wonder where he's going, and tons of scenarios infiltrate my mind. *He's meeting someone in Dell Park. He's withdrawing thousands of dollars from the bank.* Dorothy comes downstairs. Her hair is tied up and she wears a cartoonish flannel pajama set with a pair of flip flops. I haven't seen her like this since I've come here. Her hair has always hung down to her shoulders, her dress has been casual. She looks at me and smiles and I offer one back. She doesn't say anything, only moves to the next room.

"Are you okay?" I lean against the wall with one hand on my hip. I don't want to sound accusatory, but she seems a little awkward today.

"I'm fine, just decided to do a little cleaning today. You know." She pauses and reaches for something on the top of the cleaning shelf, grunting. She pulls down a feather duster and slides it over the cabinets and shelves in the kitchen and then walks to the foyer.

"Would you like some help?"

There's a small library table holding pictures of Bobby and a tableau of figures. "I'm fine. I've got it," she replies.

After dusting, she goes upstairs and I watch her as each foot clomps against the floor, sounding the alarm of her presence. I stand still, clueless as to what to do next.

The conversation at Dell Park will not loosen its grip on me, holding me like a thick chain forcing me to stand still and listen. Bobby or Anthony must have something around here that will help me know more about them. The more I talk to people, the less I seem to know about Bobby.

I creep into Bobby's room, the hinges sound. His bed is unmade, white sheets sag to the floor, his coverlet bunched to the end of the bed. I imagine him tossing back the blankets to start a new day, not knowing it was his last day. His bureau has a mirror attached to it, filled with pictures of friends tucked into the crease of the mirror and wooden frame. I approach the mirror, rubbing my hand along the side of it, smooth and cool. There's a picture of a brown skinned girl. She is pretty. No scars on her face like me. Her hair is long, her doting smile glows. There's a picture of her sitting to a cafeteria table. Another with her arms around two girls. And then there is one with Bobby, a prom picture. My eyes move to other photos on the mirror. Bobby and a white boy. I assume it is Jason. I examine the photo, trying to glean something from minute details in the background, trying to discover the hidden truths, the mystery behind my friend. I find nothing. Then I see another picture. She looks familiar. Her eyes are bright. Her hair is in a long braid that hangs past her shoulders. She stands with her hands on her hips, showing all her pretty white teeth. I get closer to the picture and realize it is Nicole. She doesn't look shy. If I had to give an analysis of her based on this photo, I would say she is brilliant, outgoing, and friendly. She looks different from the shy girl across the street.

I pull open the drawer, boxers and tee shirts are all I see. Turning around, I kneel beside his bed, getting on my knees to look under it. There's a box. I pull it out, and the dust that's traveling with it, and open it to view the contents. It's empty. Nothing. Nada. I push it back under the bed somewhat furious. *The closet. Duh!* I pause, listening for Dorothy, but I don't hear anything. I open the door. His clothes hang neatly together. Shirts together. Pants together. Shorts together. Not only that, but long-sleeved shirts are separated from short sleeved shirts. And jeans are separated from khakis. I am surprised by the organization. I never pictured him like this. I look down in the floor and his shoes are neatly aligned by name brand. Above, there isn't much, just a few of books; books I can't imagine him reading: *Make Today Count*, *It's Your Life*, *Moby Dick*, and *Invisible Man* by Ralph Ellison. A smile slides across my face when I see Ellison.

Suddenly, I hear Dorothy coming down the hall. It happens so quickly. She pushes Bobby's bedroom door open and eyes me standing in the middle of the room doing nothing. I put my hands up as if she is the police. She stares at me. She doesn't look angry, just curious.

MY KNUCKLES TAP gently against the door three times. I wait for Maria to come to the door and luckily, I don't have to repeat the knocks. She looks surprised to see me and that's understandable, meet you one time then arrive at your front door.

"Hello." Her face looks tired and frustrated. Strands of hair that have fallen from the bun, now dangle in her face. She pushes the loose strands away from her eyes. Her lipstick from this morning has worn off, leaving a thin red line on the lining of her lips.

"Hi. I just wanted to talk to you for a moment." I say it very sincere-like, hoping she will let me in. She hesitates.

"Sure. Excuse the mess," she says as I cross the threshold. Her kitchen is all white, with a marble breakfast nook. A few dishes are waiting to be cleaned, but it's not some massive mess. "Come right this way. I was going through some pictures of Jason."

She sits on the couch closest to the window and pats the empty place beside her for me to sit down. It seems so weird. She's not waiting for me to talk or wondering why I'm here. It's as if she was waiting for me to come. She picks up the open photo album from the center table and points to a picture.

"This is when he was eight years old. We'd just come from the zoo and stopped to get some ice cream." Jason's top lip was covered with vanilla cream. He smiled for the camera. She stares at the picture, hoping, with her eyes, the boy from the photo can return. This moment reminds me of Dorothy. How we sat on the patio looking through pictures and Dorothy could pinpoint exactly what Bobby was doing and where they were when she snapped the photo.

I immediately think of the look on her face when she saw me in Bobby's room. I had told her I just wanted to see it. That I'd never been in his room before and I missed him. I wanted to know what it looked like. The curious expression faded, and she smiled and told me she understood.

Maria flips the pages of the photo album. She is engulfed in the moment of each picture, a time capsule sucking her into the past. There's a photo of Maria and her husband in the center of the table. The frame is cracked, and I wonder just for a moment why haven't she replaced it, but the thought escapes me. In the picture her head is leaned back as if the laugh came from the pit of her belly. Her husband's hands are around her waist, meeting at the center of her belly with locked fingers.

"Look at this one." Maria breaks my concentration from the photo. A seven-year-old Jason stands with Daniel by a tree, holding a football, Daniel's arms around his shoulders. I smile briefly. Maria puts down the photo album.

"I have more pictures. They're in here." She signals for me to follow her.

It's almost disturbing that she has not asked why I'm here, although I couldn't have told her the truth anyway. We go to into her bedroom. Her bed is covered neatly with a black quilt and pillows colored in purple, black, and white striped pillowcases. At the end of the bed there is a black cushioned chest. A nightstand is adjacent to her bed with another wedding picture. She gives that same cheerful smile as the other one. The sheer curtains move back and forth without warning. The windows are raised slightly, and a cool breeze blows into the room. She opens her closet door and it is surprisingly messy. Pieces of clothes hang on for dear life, spilling out the hamper and dangling from hangers. Maria stands on her tiptoes as she tries to reach for something at the top of the closet. Her shirt rises, revealing a small, butterfly tattoo on her lower right side. Something falls from the closet.

"Oh shucks!" She kneels to pick up the contents. I kneel beside her, acting like I'm helping.

"This is some of Daniel's important things," she notes. "I better put this stuff back. He tends to notice when his things are moved around."

I chuckle, not because it's funny, but because I don't know what to say. She picks up the papers, shoving them into the box. I notice her wedding band. The diamond is turned slightly to the left, grazing her pinky finger.

She collects a beige document from the floor and reads it, ignoring me as if I've vanished into thin air. I lean over her shoulders slightly just to see what has caught her attention. The heading says **Insurance Policy**. I turn my head quickly before she sees me looking. She folds it up hastily and places it back into the box with other papers and shoves it at the top of the closet. She leaps to her feet and heads toward the kitchen. I follow.

"Are you okay?"

"Sure," she says, but she doesn't look my way.

"May I use your bathroom?"

"It's down the hall, second door on the left."

I leave out of her view, trying to find the bathroom, but really wanting to see Jason's bedroom. There are two closed doors. I want to open them, instead I go into the bathroom, wait thirty seconds, flush the toilet, and then run some water. I look around the bathroom, but there's nothing. I look beneath the cabinet, it's empty. Only a small container of hand soap, lotion, and a bottle of shampoo rest on the sink.

There's a knock at the bathroom door. It startles me.

"Here is some tissue." I open the door and she hands me a small roll of toilet paper. "We hardly keep anything in here anymore. This was Jason's bathroom."

"Oh okay." I quickly shut off the water and leave out after gazing around the bathroom one more time.

When I go back into the kitchen, Maria is no longer there. She is in the living room looking out the window at something. Before I get to her, she asks, "Is Dorothy home?"

"Yes. She was there when I left a moment ago."

There is a black four door car with tinted windows in the driveway. A tall, thin man approaches Dorothy's door. He raises his hand and knocks on the white framed glass door.

"Should you see who it is?"

The question doesn't register. *Why should I see who it is?* His black leather jacket makes him look important.

The man backs away from the door, looks around the yard and to neighboring houses and then walks to his car.

"I don't know who that was. Maybe a relative."

"Maybe." Maria agrees.

We both stare out the window as the car passes Maria's house and leaves Beautiful Lane.

Anthony
April 9, 2014
Morning

Anthony remained in the sunroom all morning. When he awoke he got out of bed immediately. It was as if a warning had stung him like a scorpion. He only had three days remaining to get the money and he wasn't sure how to make it happen.

Dorothy paced toward the sunroom. Quickly stepping, almost like she'd been awakened with purpose, stepping like there was hope. It was different from what he'd seen the day before. He had seen Dorothy daydreaming out the window and guessed she was thinking about Bobby. For the past few days he felt disconnected from her as if she was lost and he didn't know what to do to help her be found.

He wished he could tell her the truth about his life and why they were privileged to move in such a beautiful neighborhood. He felt his life crumbling before him, falling like a building, destroyed, debris scattered waiting to be cleaned up. One decision had become detrimental to his livelihood and he had to do something about it.

The thought of telling Dorothy the truth pierced his soul. He wanted to cry, but Dorothy peeked in at him and gave a little head nod. That was something she did to say hello, good morning, or just to say everything was okay. He smiled briefly. She had already turned away before she could see his smile. That night in Dell Park kept coming to his mind. He regretted it. He knew there was something else he should've done with the money.

His eyes watered at the thought of Bobby lying dead at the stop sign of a wealthy neighborhood. There was more he wanted to offer Bobby, so much more he wanted to teach him, but time had escaped him like a breath of fresh air. He wanted to teach him more about how to treat a lady, how to be a responsible husband and how to be a loving father.

Anthony thought about the night he was hit across the face and in that moment, he envisioned shadows moving through Dell Park, zombie-like. A tear dropped down his cheek. He wanted to do something. He wanted to make things better, but it was impossible now. He closed his eyes, took a deep breath, and paced the sunroom floor. Anthony stared out the window. He didn't want Dorothy to lose him over this foolishness. His chest tightened at the idea of him and Bobby being the price for wanting better and doing better.

THE RAIN BEAT against his car like rapid finger taps, glossing the windshield in a thick coat of water. The "H" in Hunan's Place, a Chinese restaurant, flickered several times, coming on for a full ten seconds, then flickering again. His mind raced fast as lightning. He knew what he had to do.

There was no doubt in his mind the drug dealer was responsible for Bobby's death. He paid Anthony back in the most gruesome way. Anthony could see the barrel in which the money was hidden, toppled onto the ground, no duffle bag inside.

Anthony drove through a familiar neighborhood, not Beautiful Lane, but a place where he used to live. The dark streets, dim lights, and people standing on street corners reminded him of the chaos he once knew. Most of the guys hadn't seen Anthony since he moved. They stared at the unfamiliar car that pulled onto their street.

He pulled up to two men standing on the corner. One dressed in a dark hooded sweatshirt; his hand tucked into his pockets. The other had on a baseball cap, baggy jeans and jacket. As Anthony got closer, he realized he knew them, Ronnie and Mark. They looked curiously for a moment, their hands near their sides. Anthony rolled down the window and called out to disarm them.

"Hey. It's Anthony." He remembered what they used to call him, a name he'd abandoned. "It's me, Beans." They relaxed after hearing his name and they both strolled to the car.

"Beans, what's up? We ain't seen you in forever."

They both extended their hands to give Anthony a fist bump.

"We sorry 'bout your son," Ronnie mentioned. His breath smelled like minty smoke and gold caps framed his teeth like a family photo. He and Anthony were best friends in high school, but Ronnie wanted to keep the street life and Anthony wanted to leave it.

"It's been really tough," he said. He came on that street with one purpose in mind, find out where the drug dealer lived.

Mark took out a cigarette and dramatically lit it, tilting his head forward, cigarette gripped between his lips, and flicked the lighter. He inhaled the smoke, releasing the white fog from his mouth. Mark was darker. His hair was braided back and his front tooth chipped.

"I only can assume it's hard, you know. I ain't ever lose a kid, or anything like that," Mark said. He looked at Ronnie and nodded his head to the left. A woman moved toward the streetlight. She carried a child in her arms, then stood under the light, waiting.

"Aww, man," Ronnie exclaimed. "I don't feel like dealing with her. Can you do it this time?" Mark didn't say a word. He turned around and met the woman in the cross section of the street. Ronnie stood alone and Anthony's first thought was to pry some information from him.

"So, what you been up to since leaving here?"

"Just working."

"What you doing 'round here anyway?"

Anthony's moment arrived quickly. He didn't want to appear threatening, but he needed to know the man's name and where he lived. Mark stood at the cross section. He waved his hands back and forth as he spoke to the woman. She placed her hand on her forehead like a damsel in distress.

"I need to know where the drug dealer lives that y'all work for." Ronnie's spine erected and he looked from left to right. He leaned back into the car and Anthony was sure he was going to give him the information once he saw no one within ear shot.

"Have you lost your mind?" He looked directly into Anthony's eyes. "For one, I don't even know where he lives. And two, if I did, I wouldn't tell you or anybody else, or I'd be somewhere dead. What do you need to know that for?"

Anthony thought about telling him the truth, but the truth would make it worst. "I owe him a lot of money and I want to personally take it to him." The lie rolled from his mouth with conviction. Ronnie seemed to believe it. He knew about the money that had been borrowed a few years back. He trusted Anthony. Ronnie tapped his shoes against the asphalt, thinking.

"Alright. If you get caught doing something stupid, you didn't get this from me. Got it?"

"Got it!"

"I heard his bike club will be to his house tonight. I don't know where he lives, but if you drive past the river," he pointed his finger north, "I think you will run into it. It may possibly be in the woods. I'm not sure."

Anthony looked down the street and the woman picked up her baby, placing the child on her hip. Mark walked toward the car, tossing his cigarette butt onto the ground and stomping it. Anthony was saddened for the young child for a moment, but quickly focused on Ronnie again.

"Okay, I'll holla at you later." Anthony gave him a fist-bump and drove off, knowing when he found the drug dealer, he was going to kill him for killing his son.

Jason
January 12, 2014
Morning

His eyes opened. There was no alarm, no grass cutter, or loud trucks. His eyes immediately opened, catching the sun's light swooping like an eagle across the room with each minute that passed. He was puzzled for a moment, wondering if a dream caused him to awake suddenly. Jason's room smelled fresher. Maria had come in while he was asleep, collecting his dirty laundry and putting things where they belonged, spraying mists of air freshener. He sat onside the bed, his feet greeting the cold floor. The hum of quietness filled his eardrums a light whistle that would never go away.

He kneeled to pull up the wooden tile from his floor. It was obviously loose, and he hoped Maria and Daniel didn't notice it any more than they had in the past, just a creaking floorboard. The money bag and the journal were still there. He grabbed the bag and pulled out several one-hundred-dollar bills for Bobby. A splinter jabbed his index finger, but he pulled it out quickly, dabbing the bubble of blood onto his shirt.

YESTERDAY MR. NORTON had asked Jason and Bobby for help. His hands were cold and tired from pulling the heavy bags from his garage to the end of his driveway for the garbage collector.

"Yeah," Bobby answered back. He knew how to be kind when it was necessary, but people could hardly see the other side of him, a monstrous beast waiting to pounce.

Jason went into the garage first. It was surprisingly empty. A car parked to keep the winter snow from mounting on the windshield. A pair of black gloves hung oddly on the wall by the entrance. One storage container was set on each of the four corners of two shelves that lined its way from one end of the garage wall to the next. Jason noticed how clean the floor was, almost looked like no one ever stepped a foot inside. Three trash bags were by the step leading into the laundry area, then the kitchen. Bobby grabbed two and Jason grabbed the other.

"Just put them at the end of the driveway beside the other bags."

They tugged the heavy bags and dropped them right where Mr. Norton said.

"Come inside and let me treat you for your help."

Bobby walked in first. He'd never been inside their home before. As a matter of fact, he nor Jason could recall a time where they'd ever seen either of the neighbors going into the antique style home. The storm door was white, gold color traced around an oval shaped glass with a shiny doorknob. The glossy, wooden floor was spotless, matching everything else in the house. A polished banister curved the way upstairs, each step looking like a path to something mysterious. Jason's eyes followed each stair.

108

"Come this way."

Mr. Norton led them through the living room, iridescent shades sprouting in uncommon places, purple sheer covering the mantle, yellow phone on the side table, red poinsettias under the open space of the television stand, and a fish tank radiating blue and orange from the inside. The brazen colors made the space interesting. If it weren't for the few colors springing like imaginative flowers, the room would have been basic white. White walls, white chairs, and white center piece rug.

"Linda, look who I have with me."

Mrs. Norton turned around; her eyes narrowed. "Oh, looka here," she said. She wanted to reach out to Jason, grab him by the throat and demand he'd tell her if he'd seen the little black book and where he put it, but she had to stay calm. "Would you boys like something to drink and one of my famous muffins?" She proffered.

Jason took two and smiled.

"I'll have something to drink," Bobby announced.

Mrs. Norton pulled out the container of orange juice and poured it into a glass.

"Thank you, boys, so much for helping me just a moment ago."

"No problem," Jason answered while Bobby gulped the juice.

"What sort of things do you boys do besides play sports?" Mrs. Norton asked.

"Just hang out," Jason replied.

"Hang out where? There isn't much to do around here, wouldn't you agree?"

"Just with our friends." Jason placed the muffin on a napkin.

"With your friends? I usually only see you two together most of the time."

Bobby put his glass down and looked at Jason then back at Mrs. Norton. Mr. Norton stood by the windows with his arms folded, engaged in the conversation with only his eyes. Jason always thought they were cool, one green and the other blue, but at this moment they seemed scary, leering down at them.

"Well thanks. We've got to go." Bobby took one last gulp and rested the glass back on top its circled water spot, the glass sweating like him now.

"Let me walk you to the door," Mr. Norton offered.

As they walked to the door there was something Jason noticed that he had not seen upon entering. He saw the purple sheer that covered the mantle but had not noticed what was on it. Set on the mantle were two snake statues, black mambas. He ignored it, until he gazed at two pictures on the wall and there were two more black mambas, peering their heads through foliage, venom dripping. Jason's breath was almost taken away, but he didn't want to draw attention to himself, but he knew the Norton's once lived in his house. He never suspected the book could belong to them. Until now.

JASON COUNTED THE money again to be sure what he'd taken out the bag, one-thousand dollars. He put the money into his coat pocket and walked into the bathroom. He readjusted his clothes and looked at the mirror. It was smeared. A dried soapy handprint was plastered to the very place where his face reflected.

Then he remembered yesterday afternoon, trying to wash his face and having soap lathered onto his hands, he lost his balance for some reason, leaned forward, pressing his hand upon the mirror. He wasn't drunk, or high. He was confused about the questions from Mrs. Norton and the stare from her husband. Then seeing the black mamba statues. He could feel it in his body; the random jumps in his heart rate, rapid breathing for nothing, and sweaty palms. It was all because of the journal. There were ominous discoveries that were always on his mind now.

It was 9:13 a.m. Maria and Daniel were gone. The fragrance of his dad lingered. The smell filled the hallway and traveled partially into the kitchen. He imagined Daniel sitting at the breakfast nook, adjusting his tie, reading his paper, and munching on toast before leaving for Annapolis. Daniel told Maria the night before that he was going out of town and she left a note on Jason's dresser letting him know.

Jason pulled back the curtain. Most of the snow had cleared. There were only small white patches like clustered cotton balls in shaded areas. He watched Terrell bounce the ball, dribbling it in and out between his legs. Bobby leaned his head back, holding his stomach and laughing at something Terrell said.

Although the sun shined, the cold air pushed the warmth away. Jason pulled his hood over his head and shoved his hands into his pocket.

"What up?" Bobby greeted him with their familiar handshake. Terrell only watched; the handshake was unknown to him.

"Y'all want to ball? Just one game?" Terrell asked. "Don't say it's too cold. Y'all play football in the cold." Bobby and Jason both laughed.

"I don't care," Jason responded.

Terrell tossed Jason the ball first. "Ball up!" He threw the ball back to Terrell and the game began. Bobby waited on the sidelines. The ball went in the goal, a point for Terrell.

Jason eyed Bobby and he was no longer looking at the game. Bobby was watching someone or something. Terrell bounced the ball behind his back and brought it on the other side. Jason went to the left as Terrell faked him and dribbled the ball back gracefully to the right. Another point for him.

Bobby squinted. Not the kind of squint when the sun beamed in your face, but the kind of squint where you are trying to see something, identify an object from a great distance.

"Hey, what's up?" Jason whispered. Bobby pointed down the street and Jason walked over to see what had his attention. It was Mr. Norton. He was all dressed up in a three-piece suit. They'd never seen him dressed like that before; he was always in shorts or khakis.

After Jason told Bobby about the black mamba figures and the emblem on the journal, Bobby became nervous, couldn't even sleep. "Did you not pay attention to anything around you while you were there?" Jason grieved. "I was trying to get out of there. They were freaking me out." Bobby proclaimed.

They stared at Mr. Norton for a minute, the ball bouncing in the background of their thoughts. "What's up? Are you still playing?" Jason forgot about the game, his eyes glued on Mr. Norton.

"Hey!" A female voice yelled.

Nicole emerged from the back door. Bobby and Jason stared at Nicole as she stood on the back porch, taking their eyes off Mr. Norton for a moment. Nicole wanted to get Terrell's

112

attention. Jason sometimes thought she had a crush on him because of the way she batted her eyes when he was around him. He never figured out that it was normal for her to do that once in a while, she'd bat her eyes if the sun was too bright, she'd bat them when the wind blew too hard, she'd even bat them on purpose because it was now a habit.

Jason had dreams about her that he wouldn't dare tell anyone. Him doing things to her she probably wouldn't like. Her hair was tucked in a bow, neatly in a round ball. She wore a pink shirt and a pair of black tights. He looked at her once again. Although she was younger, it didn't take away the thoughts he had towards her.

"What do you want?" Terrell yelled.

He finally realized she was holding the cordless phone.

"Momma wants you." She looked at Bobby. Nicole placed her hands on her round hips. Bobby looked at her and raised an eyebrow, smirking all the while as Terrell went to the phone. Terrell nodded his head and motioned his hands while he talked to his mom.

"Alright, I gotta do some things for my Mom. Y'all come back tomorrow if I ain't doing anything."

"Bet!"

As they trudged back to Jason's house, Jason imagined Mr. Norton saddled on top a house, his rifle aimed at his chest...no, his head, the red light marking the deadly spot. Then BANG! No warning, no sound. Just him lying on the ground with a bullet wound to the head.

The smell of his dad's cologne still lingered, but it was fading. "Did you get the money out the bag this morning?"

"Yep." He walked to his room; Bobby followed. "I was thinking we can hang out at the mall tonight. Is that cool?" Jason handed Bobby the money. He counted it quickly.

"Yeah, that's cool. We can go to the mall."

THE REST OF the snow disappeared with each drop of rain. The rain tapped against the asphalt at a rhythmic pace, steady, but light. He didn't feel excited about hanging out like he used to. He thought maybe it was something about the mood; the rain, maybe Maria and Daniel's argument that morning (which he hardly remembered), or it could've been the journal thing.

A burst of laughter came from the back seat. Dustin, another boy from the football team, showed Bobby some silly stuff on YouTube from his cell phone. They kept laughing, but Jason never asked why. It was the way he was, if someone else was laughing he'd never question why so he could laugh too, he'd let it go on and on until it stopped, never knowing the joke. They rode past Dell Park, and no one was there. The rain chased everyone back to the holes they crawled from. He imagined people moving slowly, rain tapping their feet so they can pick up the pace.

By the time they reached the mall, the rain was coming steadier. They hesitated to get out the car. Dustin received a message but shoved the phone back into his pocket.

"Are we going in or what?" Dustin asked. "Because I'm going in. Leslie is waiting for me." He opened the door and drops of rain wiggled into the car with them.

Jason watched him walk across the parking lot. He wasn't moving quickly, walking at a cool pace so he didn't look stupid in front of his girlfriend. He reached the door and Jason's eyes lost him, but he saw someone else. That someone else was familiar. The person came from a restaurant that was in the same vicinity as the mall. The walk. The clothes. He looked all too familiar. He walked with a woman. His umbrella perched above her head and his arm was thrown over her shoulder, protectively. Jason stared harder. The woman got into the car as the man stood holding the umbrella so she would not get wet. As he got into the car, the light brightened the man's face. It was Daniel, but the woman was not Jason's mom.

Daniel
April 10, 2014
Morning

Her hair tickled the tip of his nose. Her back pressed firmly into his stomach and his hand cuffed her curvy waist. She moved her hips slightly as he pulled her a little closer. She breathed deeply, then turned to face him. Her skin was smooth and honey-like. Daniel rubbed her cheek with the back of his hand, and she closed her eyes again, dazed in his presence. She enjoyed when he did that. She said it made her want to fall in love again. He wanted her to fall in love. She pushed her head into his neck, snuggling gently under him.

He glanced behind her and there was a picture of Jason. They'd fallen asleep on the sofa bed in the living room of his log cabin. He'd forgotten about the pictures that filled the living space. Twelve-year-old Jason looked at the camera as if he was caught by surprise but smiled. He was unsure how to handle his death. No one prepared him for a devastating moment like this. He didn't know Jason anymore, living with a stranger, parenting an outsider. He didn't try to know him. Jason was a lost cause in Daniel's eyes. He shook his head at the negative thoughts about his son, trying to rid them away. A picture of Daniel's father rested on the mantel. His father's green eyes scowled directly at him. The top of his flannel shirt was unbuttoned, and his brown mustache hung loosely at the corners of his mouth like untied shoestrings. Daniel's eyes were glued on the photo, but he couldn't stare any longer.

His father taught him so many things. It was his father's druthers to never let work get in the way of spending time with Daniel. His father learned to discuss difficult things with Daniel if he saw him about to make a wrong choice. When he thought of the things his father did for him, he became disappointed in himself for the things he didn't do for Jason.

His father's photo sat between two black plaques trimmed in gold, attached to a wooden frame. He managed to win the two plaques for golf, something he thought Daniel would enjoy doing as he'd gotten older. The older he got, the more distant he grew from the things his father thought he'd love. On the outside of each plaque were photos; on the left was Daniel's mother's picture and on the right was Maria's. Daniel stared at his mom's photo, just as he did his dad's. She stood by a tree in a flowered dress, smiling, eyes looking at the sky. Maria's photo was not like either of theirs. Her photo included Daniel. She had one arm wrapped around his waist and Daniel's arm was around her shoulders. They seemed happy. The picture was taken on the day of Jason's little league football game. He was only nine years old. Daniel remembered the proud moment, Jason caught the ball that spun in the air, and he ran a touchdown. Maria cheered for him. After the game, Daniel's dad asked if he could take a picture of them and quickly snapped the photo after they got into their position, smiles on their faces.

Thinking about that day made him want to be home with Maria, looking her in the eyes, thick fingers rolling softly through her hair, conciliatory. Their son was dead, and he hadn't grieved because he didn't know how to grieve. He didn't know how to cry for someone who was already dead in his eyes, someone he couldn't save. There were days he wanted to pluck him from the ground like a dying flower, wanting to put him in the safest place to nurture and water him, but it was too late. He felt horrible thinking that way about Jason, but he couldn't hide his feelings from himself. The older Jason got, the more distant they became. Long conversations became small talks, and small talks became no talks.

She moved as if she could hear his thoughts. He pushed the sheets back and slid to the edge of the bed. Her eyes were soft and beautiful. They spoke peace to him, but he knew within himself there was nothing peaceful about the situation he was in. He kissed her face.

"We must go," he said.

DANIEL PULLED INTO his driveway while Maria was pacing around in the backyard with the phone to her ear. He got out the car and Mr. Norton approached him with a casual smile. He didn't feel like talking to him. He didn't feel like speaking to anyone, except Maria.

"Hey Daniel." Mr. Norton greeted him with a handshake as usual. His palms were sweaty, but he didn't look like he'd been jogging.

"Hey. What can I help you with?"

"Well I was just coming over to check on you and your wife," he said. Daniel noticed one thing; he came to his house more than he did Dorothy and Anthony's.

"So, have you been out of town?" Mr. Norton asked as he followed Daniel into the house. Daniel gazed at his hand, remembering he'd taken off his wedding ring and didn't replace it. He could see exactly where he left it, on the table bedside the bed he shared with another woman the night before. It suddenly dawned on him what he told Maria; he wouldn't be back until tomorrow evening.

"Yes." He took a glass from the cabinet and filled it with water, guzzling it down. Daniel turned slowly. He thought Mr. Norton was staring at him - feeling that awkward sensation on the back of his neck - except when he turned around, he wasn't looking at Daniel, but glaring down the hall. Mr. Norton's eyes were fastened on an invisible object. It was as if he was beckoning something to come to him from some unknown dark place.

"You okay?" Daniel finally asked.

"Oh..uh..yeah. How's Maria?" He nodded towards the window. Daniel turned to look at her. She looked tired and frustrated. And truth be told, he didn't know how to honestly answer Mr. Norton's question because he didn't know how his wife was doing. He gave a generic answer, "She's doing the best she can."

Footsteps approached them from the hall. Daniel turned quickly. A girl stood at the arch of his hall whom he did not recognize. He assessed her. She looked young, short hair and beautiful. He noticed the scar on her cheek. She froze as if she didn't expect him, or anyone else to be in the house. They stared back.

Angel
April 10, 2014
Morning

I am crying, curled in the corner of a small room. A boy stands over me, leering. I plead for him not to hurt me. He says, "Don't worry, I won't." Then the room suddenly turns black. I can hardly breathe. I release an ear-piercing scream that causes him to crouch to the floor and grab his ears. The dream awakes me. It comes out of nowhere. I can go weeks, even months without having a single dream and then it pops up like a star hidden behind thunderous clouds.

I lay here looking at the ceiling. The vacuum hums loudly then softly as it rolls back and forth, closer to my door then further away. Dorothy's been having cleaning impulses. I stay away, not in a literal sense though. I don't want to ask too many questions or become a nuisance to either of them. Once I told Dorothy about my situation, without fully explaining things about Dan or Darla, she hasn't asked any questions about my leaving. Anthony never says anything to me. I assume he is so wrapped up in his drama that he doesn't have time to address the reason for a seventeen-year-old girl still being here.

I make my way to the bathroom, the urge to pee has gripped me like a python. I close the bathroom door hard by accident. The vacuum cleaner stops. I don't notice at first, but the quietness seems awkward. I hurry out the bathroom to head downstairs. Anthony sits in the sunroom and Dorothy walks past without saying a word to him. He has on a black panama, red sweater vest and a long sleeve white dress shirt under it. He appears to be in deep thought; he cannot see me as I peek from the steps. I wonder what he's thinking. I want to know more about what happened at Dell Park, but I can't get the information from anyone personally. Instead of coming down to greet them, I go back upstairs, jump into the shower and get dressed.

Anthony is gone before I come back downstairs.

Dorothy has on no make-up. Her skin looks soft and compliments her hair that drops to her face. I think of my day at the hair salon. *Snip. Snip.*

Although Dorothy is pretty, she looks frustrated or upset about something. A thin wrinkle rests across her forehead as she puts away the vacuum cleaner. I remember the black car from the other day. *What if it was the guy looking for Anthony?* I want to ask her about the car, instead I approach the front the door.

It is sunny, but rain clouds hover over Beautiful Lane like an umbrella. I stand on the step and see Maria's front door open. This gives me the opportunity to go over, spark more conversation with her. Hopefully more conversation than last time. I think of the insurance policy and the look on her face when she saw it. She seemed confused and after she found it her mood made me uncomfortable. An odd feeling crawls in the pit of my stomach like an animal sneaking into a pit of warning and I feel I am in for more than I've bargained for.

I KNOCK ON Maria's door. She sits in the living room, looking at something. She pushes it in the desk drawer and turns to the door.

"Hello." I say.

"Come on in." She doesn't remind me of Dorothy on this beautiful morning. She's dressed in night clothes, hair in an unbrushed ponytail. I would've assumed cleaning was the cause of her appearance if her house wasn't in disarray, different from two days ago. Boxes are lined in the hallway, stacked one on top the other. Clothes are folded neatly on two chairs in the living room.

"Excuse the mess. I'm going through some of our things to give away."

"Oh, that's fine," I say, giving a hand wave to dismiss the thought of the house being a mess. She picks up a stack of folded clothes, shirts mainly, and moves them to the hall where the boxes are. "Have a seat here." She shuffles a few things around on the desk and looks at me again. "So, when are you going back home?" A small white envelope falls to the floor. She picks it up, folds it, and puts it in the drawer. She continues to glance over other mail that's stacked on the desk.

"I'm not sure," I say. "I turn eighteen in a few days so I may find my own place." Although this is something that I'd love to do, I have no idea how I would do it. I only say it because it sounds delightsome, like I have a goal and bright future.

"Oh really!" She exclaims. "You'll be an adult in a few short days." She reminds me of Mama Wesley. How she used to search through stacks of mail, flipping envelopes over in her hand, then stacking it back into a neat collection of bills before putting them all back into a pile on the table. I think about where she put the insurance policy. *She said Daniel could tell when someone has gone in his things.* I have to get in that room some kind of way.

"Where do you work?"

"We own a real-estate business. We travel to different places sometimes. Daniel actually left yesterday morning to do a presentation for a real-estate company."

"That's cool."

"What area are you from?" She asks. I hate these sorts of questions. They make me nervous. My answers will be wrong no matter how much I try to be truthful. "I am from Hampton, Virginia," I answer. It feels good to say it. It is where the Wesley's live. I can see Mama Wesley's smile and feel her firm hugs around my neck, so approvingly. I smile at the thought of it. I hope my real mother is like her. I wish I could've stayed with them forever. I should've pretended nothing ever happened.

"I'm familiar with that area. I have a few relatives there." I hope she doesn't ask for specific areas to try to put me near her relatives. I will be stumped on that question. The phone rings. She puts down the papers and walk into the kitchen. "Hello." I imagine someone on the other end must be giving a lot of information because it takes her a while to say anything back. She walks back into the living room, hand over the receiver, "I need to take this call. Excuse me." She whispers.

"Okay."

She nods with approval and roams to the side door, then on the outside step. I look out the window and she walk toward the small shed in her backyard. This is my chance. I walk down the hall and go past the bathroom and into an open area, which leads to another section of the house. There's a laundry room and two other rooms. I open one door and posters greet me, rappers and pretty girls in swimsuits. I can picture him, or a figure that resembles him, sitting on the bed playing video games. I move around the room, gazing at the walls and ceiling as if I have just entered a palace. There is a slight chill in the room that makes me shiver upon entering. The room is a shade darker than every other area of the house and the view from his window allows me to see a murky pond hidden behind trees. The dismal ambience of the bedroom gives me goosebumps. Like the bathroom. It's not the same as being in Bobby's room. I don't belong here. An odd feeling tells me I'm in the wrong place at the wrong time.

A pair of cleats dangles from the bedpost, shoestrings locking the athletic wear together. I admire the topography Jason's seen every day since he's lived here as I stare out the window. The grass is neatly trimmed, and in the center is a magnolia tree with its skirted pedals cupping the leaves. Maria marches around the yard with the receiver to her ear, kicking grass blades from under her foot. I open the closet door first; unlike what I did in Bobby's room. I look high and low, but don't see much of anything that stands out. I'm not sure what clues I'm searching for, but I know something must be in here that will tell me something. I look in his bureau and see clothes folded and tucked neatly into each drawer.

I move toward a shelf above his bed and trip over a piece of wood that's protruding from the floor. I slide my hand across the top row of the shelf and dust particles attach to my hand like a magnetic force. I wipe the gritty substance on my jeans. I open the chest at the end of his bed, but nothing is there. I step on the spot where the wood protrudes, and it feels hollow. My eyes move back toward the floor. Kneeling, I stick my finger under the wood, raising it from the floor. There's a bag. I pick it up and shake it.

Empty. Something else catches my attention after I toss the bag back. I slide the bag over just a little. There's a little black book.

I pick it up and flip through the pages. There is writing in it. A door slams. I grab the journal and shove it into my coat, gently dropping the wood back in place. I sneak out and tiptoe cautiously to the bathroom. She's moving around, getting a glass or something. I open and close the bathroom door, pretending I'm just finishing. Something smells different, a thick odor of cologne creeps into my nostrils, then finds its way to the tip of my tongue. A briefcase leans against the wall. I hear low sounding male voices. There are two men in the kitchen. The older one sees me first and then the other glares over. One of them I recognize quicker than the other. I've seen him in the photos. It's Daniel. His blue eyes pierce the air as it does in the framed photos. The stubble on his chin makes him look mature and handsome. Daniel and the other man stare at me for a moment. It feels like forever.

"And you are?" He asks. At first, I am nervous. *How long has he been in the house? Was I in the "bathroom" too long?*

"I'm Angel. I- I've been staying with Bobby's parents." I swallow my saliva hard. He looks at me as if I'm lying. "I just came over to talk to Maria. I was friends with Bobby and I—."

Maria comes into the house, the phone gripped in her right hand. "Hey, well I see you both have met Angel." The door slams behind her and she jumps when the sound pops.

"Well, I'm Daniel." He nods in my direction, not really wanting to become friends with a teenager and all.

"Apparently Daniel's business stay ended early. I was just telling Angel how you were speaking for a major real-estate company." He doesn't nod in agreement or disagreement. He only stands there, unexplainable.

"And I'm Mr. Norton," the older guy says. He stands directly beside Daniel. His hair is slick, and his face is a little red. He smiles and stretches his hand forward. I shake it. As he leans forward, I notice an emblem on his tight-fitting jacket, a black mamba. I became obsessed with snakes one time, but Mama Wesley insisted that I abandon such foolishness and research something that really mattered. Black mambas were my favorite. They were quick. And usually didn't bother humans unless someone bothered it first. She preferred me reading novels over researching snakes. She was excited when I switched my likes.

"I've seen you around. You just came right before the..." He doesn't finish his sentence.

"I'll get going," I say. "Maria, maybe I will visit later this evening or tomorrow." She gives an unsure smile and the men say nothing. I leave the house feeling confused. Them standing there. He's supposed to be at a meeting. Her with the phone call. But I guess I've been awkward too. *Me snooping*. I walk across the street to Dorothy's and I'm glad when I cross the threshold. I hold the book tightly in my jacket, run upstairs, and plop across the guest bed. I pull the journal from my coat, believing I have found something that will give me a glimpse of Jason's life. I open it and begin reading.

Anthony
April 11, 2014
Morning

"Good morning."

Anthony awoke to Dorothy's lips touching his. The kiss was soft, apologetic.

"Hey."

He watched her blue, silk gown drop mid-thigh. He wanted to hold her longer. He wanted to say something, just anything. Dorothy stood to the bedroom window, gazing at the imagery, wondering about life, mistakes, and Bobby. Anthony only looked at her and assumed all her frustrations and preoccupied moments were engulfed around their son. What he didn't know was there was something else eating away at Dorothy, like there was something eating away at him. Anthony missed them; the them before the murders, always talking, laughing, and hugging.

He put on his pajamas, shoving both legs in simultaneously while he sat on the bed. He went to the window, hoping to see Bobby cross the street from Jason's house.

THE RAIN STOPPED, but the clouds lingered. The leaves waved back and forth with the soft wind. Anthony scanned the neighborhood. He saw Mr. Norton standing in his front yard, stretching. Mr. Norton took off in a light jog and ran past Anthony's house. Anthony admired him for a moment, envying his liberty to do as he pleased. Mr. Norton hadn't experienced any family deaths. He could continue his daily routines. Nothing had changed for Mr. Norton and his wife, whereas Anthony's life had been changed forever, dark days marked by death. There was Sharon. He watched her get into her car, leaving Beautiful Lane. Her life was still the same. She had both of her children, alive and well. Anthony felt sorry for Terrell because two of his friends were gone, but it wasn't the same as losing a child. Maria and Daniel weren't home. He assumed they had adjusted to the loss of their son. Maybe they were dealing with their grief differently. *Everyone is different,* he thought.

Anthony was startled by a sneeze. For a minute, he forgot Angel was in the house. He wondered when she was returning home. No one ever called to check on her. She never called to check in with anyone. *How is that possible for a seventeen-year-old?* He remembered Dorothy telling him that Angel didn't have a cell phone. "She lost it on her way here," Dorothy said one night as she climbed into bed. That was the only real thing she'd said that day.

Although he hardly knew anything about her, there was something interesting about her presence; there were still three people in the house. Angel's movements, footsteps, and voice filled the void of Bobby's absence. The sound of Bobby's bathroom being used wasn't missed. Dorothy still prepared food for three people, as she had been accustomed to, instead of two. Bobby's bathroom door closed, and Anthony could hear the shower nozzle turn.

He pulled the string of his pajamas tighter around his waist then tied it in a small bow. He went into his bathroom, leaving his footprint in the softness of the carpet. He thought about his conversation with Ronnie. He was right about that night. There was a motorcycle club at the house, which was not hard to find. Anthony had driven towards the river then turned on another road. The area looked vacant, dead, until he reached another point where things seemed to come back to life like the joy of spring morning. A few houses were lined on a street, but then the street darkened again. As he drove, he finally saw something in the distance. There were a lot of lights and a lot of noise, motorcycles. He wasn't crazy enough to go to his house at that moment.

Anthony eyed himself in the mirror and realized he was becoming someone he always tried to avoid. He never thought he would resort to the decision he was making. He assumed the drug dealer was after Bobby with Jason being caught in the middle. Anthony had become frustrated with police, who seemed as if they weren't doing all they could to find his son's murderer.

Bobby's bathroom door opened and closed. He could hear Angel moving quickly down the hall. By this time, he was already in his closet, reaching on the top shelf for his small safe. He placed the safe on his bed and twisted the key into the lock, removing a chrome handgun. He admired it as if he hadn't ever seen a gun, twisting it in his hand, feeling the cool metal. Anthony wondered if the drug dealer went through the same procedure before murdering his son. He dropped the gun back into the safe and locked it, putting it in its previous spot.

He saw something out the corner of his eye; it was Angel walking across the yard, headed straight for Sharon's house. He watched her cross the street, but he noticed a small object in her hand, a little black book. She did something strange though, she tucked the journal into her jacket as she reached Sharon's steps. At that moment Mr. Norton caught his attention as he jogged back on Beautiful Lane.

Terrell opened the door and she disappeared.

Bobby
January 14, 2014
Afternoon

It took him a while to register what Jason was saying. He wanted to know how he knew for sure, but all he kept saying was, "I saw him."

"Why didn't you say anything about it that night?"

"I was so angry."

"How do you know for sure it was your dad?"

"Wouldn't you know your dad if you saw him. It wouldn't matter what covered his face or what was going on. You would know your dad."

Bobby didn't argue with him on that. He understood what Jason meant and supposed he would recognize his father too if he saw something suspicious happening.

"Doesn't your dad always have business meetings? Like, what if the woman he was meeting was for a job?"

Jason shook his head, disapproving the suggestion. "No," he said. "They got into the same car and it was something about the way they were together. Walking side by side under an umbrella, arm around her shoulder."

Bobby didn't know what else to say. It sounded like cheating to him. He thought of his own parents and how he would feel if his dad cheated on his mom. Not only cheated, but if he caught him.

It was quiet for a moment. Jason steeled himself, trying to process what he discovered.

"I haven't said anything to my dad about it yet. I'm just not sure if it will come out the way I want it to," he said. "I can't believe that bastard." The last part came through gritted teeth. He paused then walked toward the kitchen and turned back around quickly. He was confused. Bobby read his face. His lips were tightened. Jason was hurt by his father's cheating and Bobby didn't know Jason cared for his mother so much.

It went deeper than his mother. Jason thought about when he wanted to spend time with Daniel before his life spiraled out of control. He remembered there was a time when he did long for a relationship with his dad, but the thought seemed foreign. Now, he blamed his father's neglect on his infidelities. He could feel himself wanting to blame his father for his own duplicitous actions. He inhaled deeply, wanting to be placid, but it wouldn't happen.

Bobby's notification sound alarmed. It was a message from Nicole. It took his mind out the frenzied environment, Jason swinging his hand back and forth, trying to get Bobby to understand.

Hi ☺. That was all the message said. Before she'd send anything else, she always sent a simple "Hi" waiting for him to respond. Bobby hadn't told anyone that he and Nicole were sort of talking, except Jason, but even Jason didn't understand the seriousness of it all. She was two years younger than him, but he didn't mind making her his girlfriend if it came to that. He managed to talk to her one day when Terrell was at basketball practice and Jason was home asleep. They laughed and talked before finally exchanging numbers, agreeing not to tell anyone.

He responded, **What up**. Jason left out the living room and came back with a glass of soda. "You want any?" Bobby shook his head, no. His phone buzzed again.

WYD?

Over Jason's. WYD?

Watching tv.

I will text you when I leave.

"What do you want to do tonight?" He asked the question suddenly.

"I don't know. It's whatever. I'll be back over later."

Before Bobby stepped outside Jason stopped him. "Quick question. Do you think we should tell anyone about you know who?" They'd been afraid to say his name after seeing the black mamba statues on his mantle and seeing him leering at them awkwardly. Blue and green is what Jason saw sometimes when he closed his eyes.

"I think you should put the journal back where you found it. Don't tell anyone and don't open it again."

ANTHONY SAT ON the couch and Dorothy snuggled under his arm. They always did this, hug on the couch and watch movies together. Bobby was used to seeing this, nothing else. He couldn't imagine his dad cheating on her, or his mom ever cheating on him.

They looked at him when he came in and gave him that gentle smile like they always did. Bobby went to his room and glanced at the pictures attached to his mirror. He remembered his mom asking him how'd he get the picture of Nicole and he told her the truth, "She gave it to me." Dorothy said nothing else about it.

Bobby took out his phone. **What u looking at?**

She didn't reply.

RINGING FILLED HIS ears. He didn't realize he had fallen asleep. Bobby cleared his throat before answering, it was parched as if his mouth was open while he slept.

"Are you coming over?" It was Jason.

"What time is it?" Although he asked, he still removed the phone from his ear to look at the time.

"Five o'clock."

Bobby paused.

"You hear me? Are you coming over?" He repeated himself. "

"Sure."

"I have something to tell you."

Bobby heard it in his voice. He didn't lilt as he'd done in past times when he had something exciting to say, enthusiasm and excitement clutching his vocal cords, squeezing out rhythmic words, but his voice was listless, disappointed by whatever he discovered.

"I'll be over soon." Bobby got up and brushed his teeth quickly. The sun was setting as the night clouds rolled in. Jason opened the front door before Bobby made it to the step. His face was tired, almost as if he'd worried himself into an older Jason.

His furious eyes were a sign that what he had to tell Bobby was not good news. With all the things that had been going on, Bobby's mind didn't draw on a specific thing that he can possibly tell him.

"I know for a fact my dad is cheating."

"How do you know?" Bobby sat on the couch opposite the television. He stretched his legs and rubbed his face. There was a picture of Maria and Daniel on the center of the living room table. They looked so happy.

"Dad came home a little after you left. Every time he comes home, he goes straight for the bathroom." Bobby frowned his face. Jason pointed in the direction of the bathroom as if Bobby didn't know where it was. "He set all of his things down in the kitchen. I'm not sure if he saw me in the living room." Bobby continued to listen. The house was quiet. The clock that ticked above the mantle seemed louder than ever before.

"Okay," Bobby said, guessing Jason wanted him to say something.

"His phone was on the counter so I hid with it by the refrigerator…you know so he wouldn't see me if he stepped into the hall." He cleared his throat as if the story was lodged there, trying to choke him. He picked up a bottle of water and took a sip. "You want one?" He proffered, interrupting himself.

"Nah! I'm good."

He continued. "I go through his phone and see a certain number that's been called several times."

"How do you know it's not for his business?" Bobby interrupted.

He puts a hand up to stop Bobby. "Let me finish. So, I see this number a few times as well as others, but this person called him, and he called them at odd times. Most calls were either placed before or after his work hours. I even saw a phone call that lasted for fifteen minutes and that was at one in the morning." Bobby nodded his head, seeing where Jason was going with this.

"I go in his text messages and there's the number again. It is not saved in his phone, just some random number. I read the messages and they said things like: *I can't wait to see you today, Had a great time last night, or It was good to hear your voice this morning.*" Jason got angry as he recanted the messages. "Dad came out the bathroom, so I memorized the number, put his phone back, and jotted it down on a piece of paper in the living room. I called the number restricted when he left, and you won't believe this."

Keys jingled and the side door opened to the kitchen. Jason peeked around the corner like the mysterious woman had come to his house. It was his mom. Bobby wondered if Jason was going to tell his mom the secret. He only spoke to her but didn't say anything else.

May 5, 2010

She threatened to destroy my life. I couldn't let her do it. She knew about the money I'd taken from the company. I had to tell her myself.
She wouldn't stop. She wouldn't back off. We saw her jogging one night. I felt the urge coming. She never saw it coming. She rolled onto the hood of the car then bounced onto the pavement.

May 9, 2010

Hector still doesn't know who killed his wife. I regret it some days, but most days I don't. She had it coming to her and I couldn't allow her to destroy what I worked so hard to accomplish.
-Angel, reading from the little black book

Maria
April 11, 2014
Morning

She had questioned Daniel. "Why are you home early from your business trip?" Maria asked after Mr. Norton left their home. Daniel folded his arms and leaned against the refrigerator, suddenly changing his mind about his communication plan. He didn't explain anything, only giving her short answers while searching the refrigerator for beer.

"It ended early." He shrugged and reached for the opener, popping the top.

"What do you mean it ended early?" She asked. He took a sip of beer and undid his tie.

"Exactly what I said, it ended early."

The lie was natural. No stammering over words. He didn't sweat about it, but she knew something wasn't right. She'd been suspecting it for too long. She didn't know how to respond to his lies anymore. She'd forgiven him in the past and she hoped she wouldn't become suspicious of every little thing, but now she was seeing those same signs again, those signs from a previous affair that she wanted to let go. She held onto the lies he told, eventually allowing them to vanish one by one like the scattering of a dandelion being blown with one breath.

But today, he thought she wasn't feeling well because she remained in bed. She was quiet, staring into the blankness of her room. Daniel peeked in. He stood at a certain angle in the hallway, so he didn't have to push the door completely open to look at her. He caught her natural beauty for a moment, something he hadn't paid attention to lately. Her hair dropped over her eye, lips slightly parted. He watched the rise and fall of her chest as she gazed the room. Her skin was without make-up. She turned her head to look out the door, but he had stepped away, making his way to the front door.

She arose as soon as he left. Showered, washed her hair, and immediately got dressed. She grabbed Jason's black baseball cap that had been in her room for a couple of weeks, shoving her hair in the cap, pulling her ponytail through the opening in the back.

Maria had a to-do-list today, but it wasn't written, it was in her mind. She needed to get more information about the insurance policy she spotted. She went to the closet and pulled down the box where she originally found it. The box was heavy, loaded with information such as receipts, business letters, and envelopes.

She saw it, the heading boldly stated **Insurance Policy**. She scanned it quickly and there was his name, Jason O'Brien Carson. She moved her fingers down the sheet, looking for more information. There was an increase in his policy. *Why would Daniel increase the insurance policy?* She couldn't remember him ever arriving home, telling her if changes had been made to the policy. She didn't know what to think about her own husband. Did she know him anymore? She took the insurance policy and shoved it into her purse and rushed out the house.

THE OPEN SIGN hung loosely on the window. The cowbell vibrated her eardrums as she opened the door. A guy sat at the front desk, thin face, pale skin, uninterested. The wooden name plate sitting on his desk said, Steve Lucas. He looked up at Maria and she noticed the scar above his upper lip, looked like stitches were once there.

"How may I help you ma'am?" Although his appearance said otherwise, his speech was sophisticated.

"I have a question about a policy on my son. Is there anyone here who can help?" He pushed some papers to the side and looked at the computer screen. He clicked once, then twice and said, "Yes, someone is here. I can see if Mr. Watson can help you."

He picked up the phone and pressed a small red button. She imagined the button calling into a secret part of the office, only the elite insurance agents, superheroes. "Can you come out front, someone has a few questions."

"He will be with you shortly. You may have a seat."

Maria sat in a green chair with wooden arms that wasn't as soft as it looked. Magazines were scattered wildly across a small table. She picked up the magazine that had a small boy on the front with PARENTING THEM printed across the top. The little boy smiled at her, but all she could see of the parent was a hand, grasping the little boy. She flipped through quickly, not ever looking at anything. A tall medium build man emerged from the doors behind the desk. His hair cut was short, and he was handsome like…like Daniel. He greeted her with an all-white smile and shook her hand.

"I'm Paul Watson. How can I help you today?"

"My name is Maria Carson." Her voice was shaky. She was afraid what she might uncover today. She reached into her purse and removed the policy. "I have some concerns about this."

He looked at it. "What's your question?"

"Well, my son was killed two weeks ago and well…this is his policy." The question she wanted to ask didn't quite make it past her lips.

"If everything clears up, you should receive the money for his death with no problem." He folded the insurance policy and handed it back to her with a smile of accomplishment on his face.

"I'm sorry. That's not what I'm asking. Can we go somewhere privately, please?"

He looked around as if there were a crowd of people waiting to meet with him. "Mmm…Sure, right this way."

The man at the desk made eye contact with her. Maria imagined his eyes following them from the waiting room through the double doors. She stepped into a neat fitting office. A nice, polished desk set in the middle of the floor. Two chairs placed side by side in front of it and another chair in the corner. The desk was neat and orderly, unlike Steve's front desk. She opened the insurance policy again, explaining her question.

"As I said previously, my son was killed two weeks ago. We had an insurance policy on him that was worth $250,000, but as you can see…" She pointed to the new amount of the policy, "His policy was increased to $500,000 two weeks before his murder. Why would someone do this?" Paul was standing, but he moved closer behind his desk to sit, unbuttoning his jacket. He gave a hand gesture offering her to have a seat as well.

"May I see the policy again?" She handed it to him, reaching over a photo of three kids, two girls and a boy, hugging each other, faces jammed together for the photo.

"What's your name again?" He asked.

"Maria. Maria Carson." He eyed the insurance policy once again and she got the feeling he was looking to see if her name was listed as beneficiary.

"Your name isn't listed on here. That limits how much information I can give you." He handed the policy back.

"So, you can't tell me why someone would do this?" She leaned forward and inhaled a gulp of air into her lungs. "Doesn't this seem suspicious to you?" She asked. When it came out, she couldn't believe she said it. The thing she'd been thinking and assuming came out her mouth, suspecting Daniel. She looked at him, but he didn't say anything in return. Maria wondered if she'd gotten Daniel into some sort of trouble, but Paul's facial expression remained stoic.

"People do things like this all the time. If they feel that people are being reckless, they may increase the policy. Sometimes people increase policies and people die a week or months later. It doesn't always mean foul play was involved. We investigate every case before distributing the money."

She leaned back into the chair feeling relieved, but not satisfied by his answer. "Well can you tell me the reason for my husband doing this?"

"Ma'am I can't give you that information. You will need your husband here to have this conversation."

She folded the insurance policy and tucked it into her purse. Paul stood to his feet, buttoned his jacket, and came from behind the desk.

"Sorry I couldn't be more helpful."

DANIEL HADN'T RETURNED home. Maria went into their room and reached for the shoebox. It slipped from her hand and the papers fell out again. She scooped them up, throwing them back into the box. She didn't care anymore. There were so many things he kept in this box; it was preposterous. A small receipt was directly on top of the stack, a hotel's name plastered across the heading. It was normal for receipts to be in stacks somewhere, he used it for tax purposes at the end of the year. She picked it up, analyzing it, hoping for some odd answer. *He traveled all the time*, she told herself.

She threw it back into the box, but then she saw another one for the same hotel, and another one. The hotel was in Alexandria, about thirty miles away from them. She couldn't remember Daniel doing business in Alexandria anytime in the past few months. The date on the receipt was January 12, 2014. She tried to think back to that week, but nothing came to mind. She got her calendar and flipped back a few months. Annapolis.

A knock at the door startled her. She threw all the papers back into the box, jamming the top onto the shoebox and stuffing it back in the closet. She fixed her hair and licked her lips. She moved quickly and swung the door open. It was Angel. It was a bad time. Maria didn't want to talk to anyone, just wanted to know the truth about her husband.

She opened the door and allowed Angel to come in.

Angel
April 11, 2014
Early Afternoon

Tomorrow is my birthday. It comes to my mind at an awkward moment as I cross the street, leaving Dorothy's house and going to Terrell's. The thought hits me out of nowhere. People usually give a countdown to their birthdays, not me. Celebrating seems foreign, alien-like, unrealistic at this point. I remember at random times how many days are remaining until my birthday, then the days escape me, never officially counting down.

I reach Terrell's yard as I see Mr. Norton jog in my direction. I slide the journal in my jacket because I don't want anyone else to see it. It feels like I'm holding the secret key to something that may later lead to something else. I wonder why this was hidden in Jason's bedroom, but that's not half as important as the information hidden in it. I knock on the door and Terrell opens almost immediately. I imagine him standing to the window, watching me as I walk out the front door, cross the street, and onto his steps.

"Hey. What's up?"

"I've got something to show you." I walk into the house and it smells sweet. I don't know if the smell is coming from him or the house itself. I stare at him briefly examining his looks. The line around his forehead, ears, and neck is evened. His lips are calling me except no words are coming from them. His brown eyes are gorgeous. He stands in the living room, shirtless, looking directly at me. The sun shines through the window, brightening his face, making his eyes brighter than they really are.

"Look what I found." I hand him the book, not cutting any corners. He opens the black, leathered journal, bound with so many secrets, and reads the first page. His lips move silently with each word. His eyes become bulbous; his mouth opens with surprise. He closes the book. He opens it again then closes it. He finally moves away from the door. His basketball shorts hang low enough for me to see his boxers. Red, white, and blue stripes. Patriotic.

"Where'd you get this?" He asks. I am ashamed to say at first. The shame turns to fear. *What will he think of me? Should I lie?*

"It was in Jason's house," I decide not to lie. He seems confused and shocked. I know what he's wondering. Why was this book in Jason's house? And how did I recover it? He sits on a long beige couch, fluffy orange pillows in each corner. It reminds me of candy corn. Mrs. Wesley used to give me candy corn all the time.

"What made you look for it?" The question hits me suddenly. I didn't expect him to ask me this. I didn't prepare for it. *What do I tell him? Oh, I think I can find out who murdered Bobby, but the clues led me to Jason's bedroom.* "I went over to talk to Maria, and it was in the bathroom," I lie. He looks suspicious but doesn't further question it. "Do you know who could've written this?" I ask.

"I don't know who wrote that, but you shouldn't let anyone else know you have it. Maybe you should put it back where you found it. You don't know who it belongs to. I think your life could be in danger from having this." He looks serious and shoves the journal back into my hands, removing the curse from his fingers. He has a point. I don't know who it belongs to, but I haven't told him the complete truth. I don't think it belongs to Maria. And why would Daniel hide something like this under Jason's floor. Was Jason capable of doing something like this. It doesn't make sense. I hold the journal in my hand, searching it over as if something new will reveal a deeper secret; a secret deeper than the contents of the journal. Who does it belong to?

I hear movement upstairs. It startles me. "Oh, that's my sister," he says after recognizing my curiosity. "She won't say anything about you being here." I stand to my feet because there isn't much else to say.

"Would you like something to drink?" He walks toward the kitchen before I can answer. I carry the book of secrets into the kitchen, its contents weighing me down like a huge rock. His bare back is attractive. *I wish you'd put on a shirt.* He bends over and grabs the orange juice from the bottom shelf and reaches for a cup in the cabinet. His body stretches and tightens. I turn away to avoid the urge to stare at him. He pours two cups of juice. I sip a little of mine.

"So, what are you going to do with the journal?"

I thought the conversation was over about that. "I'm not sure yet," I say after swallowing the last bit of juice in my mouth and waving the journal carefully.

I clear my throat thinking maybe we should talk about something else, but all that comes to mind is Bobby, my past, and other things I've noticed since being on Beautiful Lane.

"So, do you play basketball for your school?" I ask, remembering what he likes most. He smiles at me as if he was waiting to talk about basketball.

"Yeah, but the season ended in December."

"Are you really good?" I already know the answer to this after watching him the other day.

"Me?" He laughs sarcastically. "I don't mean to toot my own horn, but...you know." He takes another sip of juice and places the glass on the counter. "Do you play sports?" He asks. I wonder if he's trying to find a connection between the two of us. Truth be told, Darla didn't make me go to school. I haven't been since the beginning of the school year. She always made excuses though, because she could have gotten in trouble if my social worker found out about it. I'm not sure if I want to return to school either. I don't want to give him the real answer, so I just say, "No."

We run out of things to say again. Nicole walks around upstairs, and then a door closes. "What in the world is she doing?" He says. I shrug.

"Are you two very close?" I ask. I've always wondered about siblings. Do they really love each other the way they claim they do?

"Yeah, we're pretty close." He shrugs and drops his head.

"Do you have siblings?" He shoots back. I imagine a younger sister and brother running through the house, laughing and yelling playfully. I shake my head no and say, "I wish I did."

He glances at a photo that's behind me. I turn around to see what he's eyeing and it's a photo of him and Nicole, a younger version; chubby cheeks, puffy hair. He smiles when I turn to face him again.

"I wish I knew what it was like to have siblings."

"Well, I hope if you had any you'd be willing to do anything for them."

"I think I would." Silence falls over the room again. "I'd better go."

"Oh okay," he says disappointedly.

He escorts me to the front door. My eyes follow his spine, leading me to his shoulders then neck. He turns around to me after opening the door, his eyes looking into mine. I feel something about to happen, but I don't want to respond too quick. I don't want to look like a fool. He smiles. He moves a little closer. It feels like an anchor has settled to the bottom of my stomach. I'm afraid. I pull back and open the door.

"We'll talk later," I say.

I STAND ON Maria's step, waiting for her to open the door. The opulent neighborhood catches my attention again, it's neatly trimmed trees and beautifully styled homes. Who wouldn't want to live in this affluent community?

The black book is hidden in my jacket, clamped between my upper arm and side, causing me to move awkwardly. I don't want her to see it right now. She comes to the door, her eyes bulbous as if she's just seen a ghost. She hesitates for a moment. Her busied face is red and frustrated.

"How are you today?"

She looks around as if searching for the answer. "Well you know. I'm taking things one day at a time." Her tone is dull, uninterested. She doesn't make eye contact with me; she seems to be searching for something else, not with just her eyes, but physically.

"Would you like to have a seat?" She finally offers. I get the feeling she doesn't want company, but I need to stay. If there wasn't a circumstance like this one, I'd probably leave. She needs to know about this now. Maria walks into the kitchen without excusing herself. Glasses clatter and cabinet doors squeak. I imagine her standing on her tip toes, reaching for something far above her head. The ringing sound of marble meeting glass bounces from the kitchen to the living room. She pours something, but doesn't offer me any, then she sobs. I move slowly toward the opening leading to the kitchen. Maria tosses her head back, gulping the last bit of wine down her throat like water draining down a well.

Her shoulders shake and she wipes the tears away from her face. She pours more wine into the glass and drinks some. I want to comfort her in some way. Although I know pain, I don't know her pain. Although I've experienced loss, I don't know her loss. I manage to make my way to her and place my hand on her shoulder. She flinches as if she's forgotten I am in the house.

Maria turns to me, nervously and confused. "I just don't understand," she cries. Before I know it, her head is on my shoulder crying. Her chin presses into my collar bone and the moistness penetrates my shirt, reaching my skin. I've never consoled anyone this way before. I do what I've seen others do in movies and the two funerals I've been to, wrap my arms around her back and rub in a circular motion. I'm unsure if it works, but she seems to calm a little, then a little more, before rising from my shoulder and wiping her tears with the back of her hand.

She turns around and finishes the wine in her glass.

"Are you sure you want to do that?"

She chortles sarcastically and pours another glass and totters toward me. A plaque hangs over the counter directly behind her. It reads, A Family That Prays Together Stays Together. *Do families who really pray together stay together? Is that why my family didn't stay together?* I dismiss the questions from my head.

Maria tries to walk to the living room, but she stumbles. I catch her and walk arm in arm with her. She starts to cry again

"Please calm down. Tell me what's wrong."

Maybe it's finally hit her like a freight train, or a flotsam, the realization that her son is gone, and reality is washing up like pieces of debris.

"My life is falling apart," she begins. The journal presses in my side, acknowledging its presence in my flesh as she talks.

"Here you go." I hand her a tissue and she wipes her face and mouth with it immediately.

"I never thought things would come to this. All the pressure. All the trouble. I just don't know what to do." She folds the tissue several times, forming tic-tac-toe squares. *Does she expect me to have answers for her?* All I can do is listen. There is nothing I can say that will ease her thoughts about life. Her voice cracks and choked tears seep through her airways. She pushes wet strands away from her face. "Can you believe that bastard?"

I assume she is talking about Daniel, but I don't ask. She lends a sarcastic smile to me, tears glazing her tan face. She staggers to stand, walking nervously towards her bedroom.

"Do you need my help?" I ask. I wish I hadn't come over this moment. I want to run back to Terrell and have him stare into my eyes a little longer. A smile comes on my face, but something falls. It destroys the image. I stand to my feet quickly, wondering if she's fallen.

"Maria?"

Silence sweeps the house. I walk down the hallway, stealthily. My hand rubs along the sandpapered, white wall. Her bedroom door is open. Her bedroom smells of soap, sweet smelling soap. The window is open, and the wind blows in, the curtains dance back and forth with each other. There she is, sitting in the doorway of her closet, Indian style, back turned towards me like a three-year-old. Something is unpleasantly obnoxious about seeing her like this.

"Are you okay?"

She shakes her head. Maria sniffs the running mucus into her nostril. "I think I've found out the truth about who killed Jason." She takes a deep breath as if she can't believe she's said it. She jerks forward on those last words *killed Jason* as if a boulder dropped to her core. She pauses. "I should have known something earlier. What kind of mother am I?"

I stand to the bedroom door, listening to her complaint. Although I'm here, she looks alone, deserted. She lets out another weep, but it sounds snipped, cut off from the real source of her tears. "I found this," she says. She holds up a piece of paper. It has two, long, crisp creases that causes it to partially fold while she holds it up. I can see none of the lettering on the document.

"What is it?" I ask. She finally turns toward me. The tears have dried. She wants to say something, but nothing comes past her lips. I imagine the words coming up her vocal cords, then clogging her throat like food in a kitchen sink. She waves the paper at me, gesturing for me to get it. I walk towards this strange piece of paper, collecting it from her shaky hands. The top reads

Insurance Policy, like I'd seen before, in thick bold letters. She wants me to look at it. It feels like a frog has jumped in my throat, a lump that won't go away. There was Jason's name on the policy. It looks foreign as if I had never seen the name "Jason" written anywhere else. Even if I had, this Jason is dead. The policy is worth $500,000. Someone will or has collected this money.

"How are you connecting this to his murder?" She looks at me with grievous eyes. She motions back and forth, the alcohol having full effect now.

"Daniel did that," she slurs. I was unsure what the "that" was.

"What are you talking about?"

"Daniel is the beneficiary of the insurance policy."

I'm confused by her statement. Parents are usually the beneficiaries of their children's insurance policy. How did she conclude who killed Jason based on Daniel being the beneficiary? Maria stands to her feet, still trying to articulate more words, but the alcohol will not allow it.

"H- He killed our son." The words slither through tight teeth. Her eyes narrow, her lips curl.

"How do you know?" She stumbles a little to the left, making her way to the bed.

"Why else would he increase the policy two weeks before Jason was murdered?" My expression changes. I can feel my nose wrinkle, my eyebrows frown. I thought the policy was an original. There was no way for me to know he increased the policy. She rocks back and forth on the bed in confusion. Her hands are placed on her head. I look at the paper, the seal of death in my hand and wonder why a father would increase his son's policy right before he was murdered. I get nervous, hoping Daniel doesn't come home while I'm here. I sit on the bed beside her and she cries in my arms, again.

I THINK OF Terrell when I walk out Maria's bedroom, into the living room. I imagine him hugging me, showing me affection in a way I'd never felt before. I'd seen people hug, kiss, and hold hands, but I'd never experienced it myself. Has my scar kept others away from me, or did it keep me away from others? His brown eyes, his broad shoulders, are all I see in my mind.

Maria emerges from her bedroom, stretching her hands over her head, her belly button and pale waist peeking out under her shirt. She had fallen asleep after all the crying earlier. I'd attempted to placate her by telling her Daniel had nothing to do with this, it's all a misunderstanding, but she rested her head in my arms, cursed Daniel, cried some more, then the next thing I knew she was asleep. I wanted to leave, but I didn't want her to be alone, all the time afraid of Daniel's arrival. She looks at me embarrassingly, but I smile. She picks up a glass from the counter, runs the tap water and fills her glass.

"Do you feel better?" She glares out the kitchen window into her backyard. Her eyes are on the wooden gazebo. She stands quietly to the window, putting the glass of water to her mouth, only sipping enough to wet her lips. "Are you okay?" I ask, genuinely caring.

"NO!"

Then without warning exclaims something. "I even think he is cheating on me." She says it as if she is not talking to me, but to someone outside the white framed windows. I look at the time, it's 6:42. The sun highlights the backyard and light screams through the window. I squint to look past the sunlight and at Maria. I don't know what to say to her though. I feel like the journal in my pocket means nothing. I think of Bobby's parents after the revelation Maria has gotten concerning the murders. What will Dorothy think about this? What will Anthony do to Daniel? Will he kill him, or report him to the cops? Then my mind shifts back to Maria, *if she believes Daniel has something to do with Jason's death, why hasn't she called the cops.*

She walks away from the window, the sun gradually setting. Maria disappears into her bedroom again, the dim light swallowing her whole. I hear the closet door screech open. She comes out the bedroom fully dressed, blue jeans, and white shirt with fancy lettered words written across her breast, and a pair of sneakers.

"Would you like to take a ride with me?" She asks. At first, I am a little confused. She doesn't seem like herself.

"Sure," I hesitate.

"It will be fine," she replies. Her voice still sounding a little foggy from the alcohol.

"I can drive for you." I say. She doesn't seem sure about it, but then agrees.

The sun hides its face behind the trees, vanishing in time. Darkness has arrived. We get into the car and I see Terrell's bedroom light on, at least that's the one Sharon pointed to when we talked in the yard. There are no lights on in the Norton's two-story monster. For the first time it looks as if claws are tearing from the sides of the house with horns ripping through the roof. I pull out the yard, looking both ways carefully. Another car turns onto Beautiful Lane. It creeps down the road slowly, suspicious. It looks familiar and suddenly it hits me. It's the same black car that Maria and I saw pull into Dorothy's yard the other day. I glance over at Maria, but she's looking out the passenger window, glassy eyed. The car approaches me, and we drive past, looking each other directly in the face as if he is looking for me and I am looking for him. I stare in the rearview mirror and sure enough, the car pulls into Dorothy's yard.

Mr. Norton
April 11, 2014
Morning

He awoke at such an awkward time; 5:43, a little before his alarm sounded with a loud tune. The room was dark, but there was a hint of light peeking through the curtains. He lay still for a moment, feeling Linda's back crouched against his, her deep, rhythmic breaths, irregular to his. Linda shifted her body, making low throat-clearing sounds.

He thought of his little black book. The things that were written inside made the hair on his neck stand. He stared at the ceiling. *What if someone has read my deepest secrets?* He couldn't imagine what they'd do with the journal. *Show others? Take it to the police? Blackmail him?* Beads of sweat bubbled on his forehead. All the secrets that were bound in the book made him want to choke. It wasn't just Hector's wife. There were more. The man from Pennsylvania who stole from his parents when he was only twenty-three years old. The graduate student who he'd invited to his apartment and when she called him a creep, he beat her in the head with a lamp, then drove three hours to dump her body in

157

the woods. He was twenty-nine years old. There were at least three more. All written in the book to relieve his mind.

Linda turned again and he knew she was going to awake soon. That's what she did when her body told her it was time to rise. She'd fight it for a few minutes, opening and closing her eyes, moving about in the bed, before finally awaking completely.

HE POURED THE water into the coffee pot.

"Good morning," he acknowledged first.

She smiled and said the same. Linda opened the refrigerator door that was covered with photos of their children and grandchildren, a lifetime of events: babies first pictures, soccer, baseball, family time, and beautifully drawn and colored artwork. Those moments captured and put on display in his kitchen reminded him of something that didn't exist for him, a secure life. They hadn't seen their children and grandchildren in two years. They lived so far away. Linda's hand rubbed mistakenly across one of the photos as she walked to the sink.

"I put the coffee on," he notified.

"I see." She turned a knob and the water rained out of the faucet. She looked peaceful as she stood to the sink, but deep down inside she was worried. There was a constant nagging in the pit of her stomach like someone pulling at strings.

"What are you doing today?" He asked. She stood to the counter, spreading strawberry cream cheese onto her bagel. She wished within herself she'd never learned about her husband's real job. It was all an accident, stumbling upon information that she was never meant to discover.

"I think I'm going to clean out the closets. They're getting a little crowded." What she really wanted to do was go to Maria and Daniel's home, search the house wildly, removing things from the cabinets and searching closets from top to bottom to find the black book. She bit the bagel and a dab of strawberry cream cheese rested on the corners of her mouth. She licked it clean.

"What are your plans?" She asked.

He didn't know how to respond to her question, because he knew exactly what he wanted to accomplish, getting his journal back. The sun shined completely into their kitchen now. A beam of light waved across Linda's lips and right cheek. His eyes followed the beam of light that crawled across the kitchen floor and brightened the pictures of his children.

"I want to get my journal back. I don't know how, but that's what I need to do." He saw the hope in her eyes, like a child expecting something good to happen today. "I just really think it's time that I am aggressive about finding this."

She shook her head in agreement as she chewed the bagel, taking a sip of coffee afterward.

HIS FEET PRESSED against the asphalt as he took off in a light jog down the street. The jog freed his mind, made him feel less tense. He thought of ways he could retrieve his journal. The simplest thing he could do was just ask for it, tell Maria or Daniel he left something in the house when he moved out and he knows where it is hidden. But he crushed every idea that came across his mind like pebbles under his feet.

Sweat trickled down his back as he turned off Beautiful Lane and continued on another street. He wanted to crush Linda's worries, but there was only one way to make that happen. He thought about talking to Daniel again, after all, that was the purpose of his last visit, but when he saw Angel, it thwarted his plan.

A sound startled him, almost causing him to lose his balance. It was Sharon. She honked the horn again and drove past him as he gave a happy wave.

He jogged for a shorter amount of time today. He wanted to return home to tell Linda of what he could do to retrieve the book. A cool breeze blew into his face. He was almost at Beautiful Lane before his leg muscle tightened and he stopped immediately. He hadn't gotten a cramp in years. He rubbed the back of his leg to ease the pain. Mr. Norton straightened himself and walked back and forth, bending his leg to relieve the tension.

When he reached Beautiful Lane, he saw Angel. She bounced as she walked across Anthony's yard. He thought about how young she was, and he imagined his daughter being that age. He missed out on so much and it haunted him. Everything that caused him to miss out on his children's life was wrapped in a little black book.

He picked up speed a little bit to catch up to her. He wanted to say hello or say something that would help their unlikely meeting at Daniel's house. The cramp left his leg. He felt better and could jog at his normal speed. She reached Sharon's yard and he knew he would not make it to her in time. *Maybe I'll speak to her later,* he thought.

For some reason his eyes were fastened on her. He wanted to look somewhere else, but he couldn't. She held something in her hand he thought was familiar, but it couldn't be what he thought. His eyes were fixed on the object. It was a black book. At first, he thought he was seeing things, his mind so focused on the book that he was beginning to imagine it. Suddenly, his jaw dropped. He saw Angel look in his direction and tuck the object into her jacket, as if to hide it from him. He wanted to run to her, explain the truth about the book. He found himself out of breath, wanting to reach out to her, but Terrell opened the door then she was gone; closed behind the door with his journal hidden secretly in her bosom.

HE STUMBLED IN the house, trying to find Linda to tell her what he'd seen. He rushed through the living room and heard her panicked voice behind him. "What is it, Harold?" He came into the house so fast he didn't see her sitting on the couch watching T.V. Her hand was on her chest and her mouth partially opened.

"What is it? Tell me."

He threw his hands up wildly, trying to catch his breath. "I think I saw my journal," he spat.

"What do you mean you *think* you saw it?" She scratched her head then folded her arms as if Mr. Norton was about to drop some fantastic story on her.

"I saw that girl...Angie...I mean Angel."

"Who?"

"Angel. The one that's staying with Dorothy and Anthony."

"Okay you saw her. What does that have to do with anything?"

"I think...," he corrected himself, "I saw my journal in her hand. When she saw me coming down the street, she hid it in her jacket. I saw her do it. I'm serious." Linda didn't say anything right away.

"Are you sure?" She finally questioned. For some strange reason it crossed his mind that Linda wasn't cleaning out the closet like she said. That's why he ran past her because she was supposed to be cleaning, not watching television. The thought left.

"Yes. I am sure."

"Where did she go?"

"She's to Sharon's right now. I need to get my journal as soon as possible."

Not too long after their conversation, they saw Angel walking to Maria's. He imagined her taking the little black book out and showing the contents of the journal to Terrell, little Nicole, Sharon, and now Maria.

MRS. NORTON DIDN'T talk much. She'd gone off to herself, shuffling with papers on the table, walking to the closet and only looking in, but never touching anything.

"Why are you sitting here? Are you going to do something about this?" She asked impatiently.

"I don't want to go over there while she's in the house."

Linda glanced out the window, moving the curtains carefully to the side, trying to see Angel emerge from the house. She'd been in Maria's house all day and they were sure she would've left by now.

"Harold, they're leaving," she panicked, "both of them are leaving together in Maria's car." She glanced at the time. Seven o'clock.

He jumped to his feet, hoping he could seize this moment to go into Maria's home. He hoped Angel left the book; maybe she didn't want any parts in the mess. *What if they are going to the cops with the journal? What if they've discovered who it belongs to?* A punching pain hit his gut.

"I'm going over now." He stood to his feet and headed for the back door.

EVERYONE'S YARD WAS dark, nothing shined. The clouds covered the light the moon had given. He ran through the dewy grass, making his way to Maria's backyard. The sound of wild bugs and creatures by the pond infiltrated the air. He eased his way to the dining room window; it was framed with painted white wood. The look changed since he lived there.

He pushed the window up and discovered it was unlocked. He pushed a little harder, widening the crack, making it big enough for his head and shoulders to fit in. He took one good jump and his upper body was in the window. Mr. Norton slithered through, falling to the floor, breaking nothing in her house, or on his body. For a moment, he saw his old house, the way it was decorated and how the furniture was placed, the photo of his two daughters, hugging each other tight about the neck with wide smiles, his baseball cap sat on the rack leading out of the kitchen, Linda standing there waving it to him before he left the house. Then he saw the real house, Maria and Daniel's house, not his.

He moved down the hallway, removing a small flashlight from his right pocket, going straight for Jason's room. The bedroom door creaked open when he twisted the doorknob. He kneeled immediately, putting the flashlight in his mouth so he could use both hands if necessary. The wood came out the floor as easy as he remembered. Mr. Norton moved the flashlight back and forth, looking into the corners of the hidden area. It wasn't there. All he saw was a blue duffle bag. He picked it up, shook it. Nothing. Disappointment greeted him like a sour taste. He knew now that his thoughts were right about Angel. She had his journal. He imagined her recovering the book on that day he met her at Daniel's house. Taking the book from the floor and bitterly reading its sour content. The light shined around the room, bouncing from the floor to the wall, as he stood to his feet. He put the wood where it belonged, left the bedroom, and imagined how dissatisfied Linda would be when he returned empty handed.

Jason
January 14, 2014
Evening

For the first time, Jason felt guilty about something, knowing that his dad was cheating and not being able to tell his mother. He picked at the pimple on his chin that turned red and flaky, annoying him. He thought about the long nights Daniel told him he was working. Anger boiled over in him. He suspected that every time his father wasn't home, he was with her. Jason sat on the couch, propping both feet on the glass table, gently tapping a picture of Daniel and Maria with his shoe. He wanted to placate himself, thinking of something fun, watching television, but neither worked.

He asked Bobby to come back over so he could tell him all that he discovered about his dad. He hated his dad right now. He knew that he himself had not been the best son, but he had no idea that his mother was carrying the weight of her two closest men being a disappointment to her. Bobby walked in the house again. After waking suddenly to Jason's phone call, he saw a return message from Nicole. He didn't have time to respond now. He wanted to know what Jason had discovered and why Jason felt it was important to tell him.

"What's up?"

"Nothing much. Just want to finish telling you what I know."

"Where's your mom?"

"She's in the room…sleep I think, so don't talk loudly." He put his hand in front of his mouth as if he was making too much noise.

"So, what is it?" Bobby asked. This time Jason put one finger to his mouth as if he was too loud, but he wasn't. Jason waved Bobby into the living room. He turned up the volume on the television. A tall white man had on a tuxedo, holding a cordless microphone. He looked nervous before opening his mouth and releasing melodic tunes, but neither of them paid attention to the show.

"Remember how I was saying I looked through my Dad's phone right?"

Bobby nodded his head. His eyes were watching Jason's lips so he could fully understand each word.

"I called the number back and no one answered." Bobby looked at him disappointedly, wondering how in the world he knew for sure his dad was cheating if he hadn't talked to anyone. Bobby's phone vibrated in his pocket. He pulled it out and there was another message from Nicole. He tucked the phone back into his pocket and continued listening to Jason.

"The voicemail came on and it was Sharon, Terrell's mom." Jason was finally glad to get those words out his mouth.

Bobby's eyes, bulbous.

166

"Can you believe my dad? Sharon is my mother's friend or...I mean they talk a lot, but she's sleeping with my dad." He felt the tension rising to his throat, spewing over like hot lava. He pressed his fist into the table, but he wanted to bring his fist down with force, smashing the glass.

Bobby only stared at him. Not sure what to say next. He watched Jason's face, cheeks, and the round of his ears turn red.

Jason wanted to hurt his dad. Jason wanted to hurt Sharon.

Angel
April 11, 2014
Late Night

After driving for an hour and a half, we arrive to a cabin in the woods. The entire ride was tense, filled with long moments of silence mixed with burst of chatter. She hadn't told me exactly where we were going, but she mumbled things to herself about Daniel and I cringed. I guess she didn't think I heard her, but at one time she said, "He thinks I'm crazy. I've got something for him." I didn't want to be a part of this, but I needed to find the truth. Who killed Bobby? Did Daniel have anything to do with this? I could feel the anger rising like the temperature of warm water, one more degree and I'm boiling hot. My hands tightened around the wheel. We reached a dark area, surrounded by tall trees. No streetlights helped to light the way.

"Where are we going?" I had asked. Maria didn't answer my question, she simply said, "I am sweating." It sounded so odd coming from her at this very moment. I rolled the window down, releasing the warmth. The wind pushed her hair from her face with force. We stopped at a stop sign, hearing the hiccups of frogs and the creaking of crickets.

"I need to see something for myself." She didn't give an explanation. I wanted more details. I needed more details.

I looked at her, my right hand placed on the gearshift. The smell of her perfume bounced around the car, hitting my nose viciously. I felt a sneeze come on, but held it in, letting a tiny squeal come past my lips.

"Turn here," she said.

I turned down a dark road, surrounded by more grass and trees. A possum darted in front of the car and I slowed just a little. We kept on the road for fifteen minutes. It was the oddest experience in the car I've ever had. I wondered how I got to this point. I want to know who killed my friend, but I am in a car with a woman, whom I barely know who is looking for God knows who and what. We drove down a smooth road and suddenly I heard tire crunching pebbles, the road secretly turning to gravel.

"Make a right here." I could tell she'd been here quite a few times. She told me to turn when I could not see a place to turn. I turned down another lane and drove deep into the throat of the woods. Green eyes peeked from behind trees and limbs. Finally, we came to a lighted area.

The driveway is covered with rocks and divides at a certain point, making a complete circle around some lighted sculptures that sit in the middle. Beautiful plants surround the sculptures and white stones border the plants. I pull the car closer and the headlights move briskly across the front porch. I press firmly on the brakes and the car comes to a complete halt. We are here, sitting in the driveway, not saying a word to each other.

"Put the car in park," she says. Anger thunders off her tongue, rumbling through the car. A light is on. I can see it dimly shining through the slits of the blinds. Maria hesitates.

"Are you getting out? Is Daniel here?" I hope she will respond to both questions, but she only glares out the window. The porch stretches from one end of the log cabin to the next. Two glass windows are fixated above the porch roof like two perched eyes. Maria puts her hand on the door handle.

"I have to know for sure." She opens the door and I hear gravel moving under her feet.

"I'm going with you," I say. I'm not going because I want to, but it is creepy out here and I don't want to be alone in the dark. I open the door and immediately hear chimes beating against each other, moving carelessly with the wind. We both gently close our doors, hearing only a click of door connecting to metal. The smell of fresh grass penetrates my nose. I rub my hand against the oak railing, balancing myself in the dark. Keys jingle. I'm not sure whose keys because I left Maria's keys in the car. Then I see Maria retrieve a set of keys from her pocket, pulling back the storm door and wiggling the key into the hole. For a moment I cannot distinguish the sound of the keys from the chimes clanking, they become as one. A hint of blue light outlines the front door. Maria pushes it open slowly. The television is on, lighting the living room a mysterious blue. A tall man is dressed in a tuxedo holding a microphone. He is singing and the camera pans across the crowd. They are clapping for him. I remember seeing this episode at Darla's house a few months ago.

The cabin smells of fresh vegetables, and some spicy oil. I know that oil. It is familiar. My mind goes back to the moment, inhaling the fragrance into my nostrils and loving it. Then I remember, Terrell smelled like this earlier today. There are pictures sitting on the side tables and lamps placed carefully behind them. The mantle holds several things, pictures and plaques, but I cannot make out who are in the pictures. Maria is a little distance ahead of me now. She knows exactly where she's headed. I walk a little faster, catching her as she reaches the step. The steps aren't creaking, and I can't hear the television anymore. We reach the top and there is a faint sound coming from behind one of the doors. Maria looks at me. Appalled. She moves to the bedroom and places her ear to the door. Someone giggles.

Maria opens the door and for a minute I think we have stumbled into the wrong place. Maybe Maria didn't know where she was going after all. Maybe she came into the wrong cabin, but then I remember the key. She came in with a key. She knew twist and turns to the house that no one else would know except they'd been here before. *Why is Sharon here?* I see someone dart from the center of the bed leaving Sharon sitting there, looking surprised. Although the scene doesn't register at first, I realize it is Daniel. He's in his boxers, looking frail and handsome. At once, Maria charges the room, bouncing across the bed and tumbling over into the floor with Sharon wrapped into her arms. A thud strikes the floor. Screaming! A lamp falls, shards of glass around them. I look at Daniel and he's frozen, shocked by Maria's entrance.

"Aren't you going to do something?"

I hear a voice yell, "How could you?"

"Get off me!" Sharon yells. Maria rises a little from the floor, but I see her fall furiously down on Sharon. Maria kicks Sharon backwards and she hits her head on the small table next to the bed. Daniel finally rushes over, holding both hands awkwardly as if he doesn't know who to grab first. Maria stands, but stumbles backwards. Her hair is wild and so is her face. She's red, her lip is bloody. Her shirt hangs off her shoulder. Sharon gets off the floor and scoots across the bed, gathering her clothes from the floor.

Blood stains her inner thigh and forearm. Scratches cover her right cheek and her lip is swollen. She scuffles past me, holding the clothes tightly.

"How could you do this?" Maria yells in Daniel's face. She pounds on his chest as he tries to grip her hands.

"I can explain," he says. *Classic line.*

She snatches away from him, yanks me by the arm, saying, "We need to leave. We need to leave." We reach the front door and I see glowing trees. A light zones-in on the trees every second. The sound of gravel under tires is in my ears again. It's Sharon, speeding out of the driveway. She was parked behind the cabin and I assume Daniel's car is back there too.

Maria gets in the car and slams the door. I do the same. I start the car and she turns to me, bursting in never ending tears. I pump two deep puffs of my inhaler into my chest.

BEAUTIFUL LANE SEEMS creepy tonight. The moon is hidden from us. The trees lean in as we ride past, its branches hunch over, clawing at the road. Maria has stopped sobbing. Her cell phone rings. Blocky white letters appear, but I don't read it. She looks at the screen and swipes her finger in the direction of the red arrow. She tucks the phone back into her pocket. I assume it is Daniel. I imagine him sitting on the edge of the bed, still in disbelief that his infidelity has been exposed. I touch Maria's hand to remind her I am still here. Her hair and clothes tousled. So was Sharon's. I feel sorry for Maria.

Bright lights shine in our direction, a car parked on side of the road. The lights are too bright for me to determine who it is. I pull into Maria's driveway, feeling the awkwardness for her. Her son was just murdered, but her husband is out having an affair. He's continued to work. He's increased the insurance policy. Wild things run through my mind about this guy I barely know, only met him twice. Both awkward occasions. I look up the street, only a short distance, and now I can see the car. It is parked in front of Dorothy's house. I glance at the time and it is only 10:14. It feels so much later. The drama has slowed the time. Anthony and Dorothy stand on the porch.

Maria gets out the car and slams the door, her shirt still hanging slightly off her shoulders, evidence of the incident. Loud chatter moves across the street like warning signals. Maria ignores it. I hand her the keys and she go into the house, saying nothing to me. The car parked at Dorothy's house is the same black car I saw a few hours ago.

"What is he talking about?" Anthony yells. I make it to the front yard and there's a tall guy, who looks taller than Anthony, standing at the bottom of the steps. He has on a black jacket and light blue jeans. He looks calm, unworried. Dorothy glances at me with embarrassment. I remember the conversation that Anthony has had on the phone. I remember what the man in Dell Park told me. Is this the person that Anthony was attacked by? Does he know something about Jason and Bobby? I want to piece it together in my mind like small pieces of a puzzle, but I can't make the connection, nothing fitting well together. I look at Terrell's house. Sharon's car is there. Terrell's light is off. I wish I can go over to see him. Dorothy tries to get out some words, but they continue to trip over her tongue.

"I've been looking for you for years. Why didn't you tell me?" The man says.

"She didn't have to tell you anything." Anthony makes a move toward the bottom step, but Dorothy grabs his arm. Maybe I should go into the house, stay out of this whole mess. I've been involved in too much for the night.

"You know nothing about Bobby," Anthony yells back. I have a flashback when Bobby's name is mentioned. We are laughing in a park; he's pushing me in a swing. He laughs and I say something to him. "You didn't tell me happy birthday, yet." He stops the swing from going higher and then brings it to a complete halt. I turn to him and he smiles. "What?" I giggle back.

"Happy birthday. I didn't forget about it. I just didn't want to say anything yet, knucklehead." He pushes the swing again and I laugh louder.

"He's my son," the tall man says a pitch higher than Anthony, pulling my imagination back into reality.

Anthony tightens his fist. He looks at Dorothy. His face is distorted, not looking like himself. "Dorothy how could you not tell me this?"

All she could squeal out was, "I'm sorry."

Anthony stomps down the steps, staring the guy eye to eye before he moves my way. I don't know if Anthony notices me or not, but he bumps right into me, causing me to stumble backwards. The journal shifts in my jacket. The words I've read swirl in my head. Anthony gets into his car and speeds down Beautiful Lane. It is not until Anthony leaves that I know the real reason for the man coming to Beautiful Lane. His face is round, with a fitting chin. His lips are naturally puckered, but he is handsome. He looks at Dorothy in all seriousness and says, "Where is Bobby? I want to see my son."

Dorothy's hands go up to her mouth in shock and I stare in disbelief. I cannot imagine how she is going to break the news to him that Bobby is dead. I finally turn away, leaving them outside alone.

Daniel
April 11, 2014
Evening

Each time Daniel was with Sharon it made him forget about Jason. It sounded bad when he thought about it that way, but it was the truth. He wanted to run away from everything that seemed familiar, wishing he could take a flight of stairs to the moon, feel his back press against the hard element, become a resident. He couldn't sit there like Maria, whose entire being was wrapped into Jason's death like a warm blanket. He thought about their night in Florida, him hugging and kissing her after his presentation and her giggling and rubbing her hands through his hair.

Daniel had to leave the house and he wanted to be gone as long as he could. Everything in his house reminded him of Jason. His clothes, his room, his shoes that set by the kitchen door waiting to be filled with his feet. Daniel noticed the mud around the soles of Jason's shoes before he walked out the house. He had no thoughts about where it had come from; he just wanted to get past them as quickly as possible to see Sharon.

He met Sharon at the log cabin. Daniel gazed at Sharon from the back porch as she emerged from her car, putting her legs out first, showing the red heels that hugged her feet. She was dainty like the rose pedals he sprinkled across the bed for her. She swayed her hips from side to side with each step. Daniel imagined

176

Sharon's sweet and soft skin under his fingertips before she reached him. Sharon paused in front of Daniel and touched his waist gently, tugging on his blue polo shirt, the shirt he'd forgotten represented a bond between him and Jason. Jason bought matching shirts two Christmases ago, hoping it would help Daniel become more interested in him. It didn't work.

Sharon kissed his face, then lips. Her hair hung loosely to her shoulders as he rubbed his manly fingers through it. Her red lipstick made her more attractive. Daniel tucked his fingers between hers and escorted her into the house.

"It smells good in here," she said as she rubbed Daniel's arm. "What did you cook?"

"Steak with sweet peppers and fried rice."

She smiled and that did something for him inwardly. His heart leaped, butterflies filled his stomach, and he could feel the blood flow through his veins again. Maria never smiled anymore. He had to witness her tears and truth be told, her tears hurt him more than his own. When he was with Maria, he had to see where he failed, but with Sharon he was not a failure.

Sharon sat down to a candle lit dinner. The flames belly danced back and forth over the wooden table, creating a tableau of shadows on the wall. Daniel sat across the table and Sharon extended her hand for him to caress. He rubbed his thumb along the curve of her index finger and thumb.

"Taste the food. I think you'll like it."

She cut the steak easily and placed her lips around the utensil with her eyes on Daniel all the while. She gave an approving head nod. She stood from the table and held his hand.

"The food is wonderful, but let's go upstairs," she said. Daniel moved around to the other side of the table where Sharon was now standing. He grabbed her hand, kissed it.

He turned off the lights and blew out the candles. The television was still on, lighting their adulterous path up the steps. They reached the bedroom and he could not control himself in her presence. She wasn't fragile like Maria. She wasn't heartbroken. He didn't need to ask if it was okay to touch her. He missed that about Maria and he wanted to make things right with her before Jason was murdered, but the pain of his death wouldn't let him do it.

Dorothy
April 12, 2014
Early Morning

Night and day seemed to mush together as one, making time unidentifiable since the incident the night before. She felt like she was at the bottom, the bottom of life, everything collapsing and crushing her. Anthony didn't return home and she worried about him. She picked up her cell phone and dialed his number, pressing each finger firmly into each button. A mechanical voice pricked her ears. She wanted him to return her call, tell her where he'd been. *I went to the lake to think for a little while,* she imagined him saying.

The unwrinkled sheets and neatly placed pillows next to her caused her to feel broken. No back to rub against. No feet to intertwine with hers. No arms holding her hips. She got up and wrapped the plush-like robe around her waist as she walked to the window, hoping to see him move pleasantly to the front door. She opened the blind and there was no one.

The sun painted hints of pink across the sky as the sun rose on the east, long, thin clouds floating across the dazzled sun. Dorothy admired its glow before turning to hit redial on the phone.

It was the same automated lady that she'd heard so many times last night. This time the voice angered her, and she chucked the phone onto the floor. She yanked the bedroom door opened and spotted Angel. She was on the steps, elbows resting on her knees, hands cupping her chin.

"Are you okay?" Dorothy asked, leaning her head to the side in that caring manner.

"I guess."

"Would you like some coffee? Breakfast? Anything?"

Angel looked at Dorothy and shook her head, agreeing to one of the options. She followed Dorothy into the kitchen. Bobby's photo hung above the countertop and Dorothy imagined Angel staring at it as she sat to the table. *BobbyBobbyBobby.* She said his name repeatedly as if she had to remind herself of his presence, not wanting to let him go.

Dorothy traipsed toward the steaming coffee pot, removing it from the coffee maker, pouring coffee into two small mugs. It was her druthers to mix vanilla cream and two teaspoons of sugar into the coffee, watching the hypnotizing swirl. She sat in front of Angel, but Angel stared past her, then broke the silence.

"You sure you're okay?"

"Yes. It's just…" The words were knifed abruptly. "I feel lost," she began again. "I don't know what I'm doing anymore."

"What was going on last night? I'm so confused."

Dorothy dropped her head. She didn't want to explain her careless mistakes to a teenager; yet, she felt like she owed her something. She inhaled deeply and tears welled up in her eyes. She brushed them away with the back of her hand, but not before one managed to roll down her cheek and land on the table.

"It's a long story," Dorothy began. Angel didn't respond. Her face said a thousand words. She didn't care how long the story was, she just wanted the truth.

"How could I have been so stupid? It was one mistake." She gripped the mug with both hands after taking a quick sip. The hot taste buzzed the tip of her tongue.

Angel cleared her throat, unsure how to respond.

"He came by and told Anthony everything before I could tell him myself. I'd been trying to figure out how to tell him the truth."

Angel drank some coffee then put the cup back down. Dorothy glanced at the mark on her cheek and continued. "I don't think Anthony will ever forgive me."

"So, this man is telling the truth? He is Bobby's father?"

Dorothy nodded her head, yes.

"He said he was coming to see Bobby. He didn't even know Bobby was killed last week.

"He just happened to pop up the week after the funeral looking for him? Isn't that weird?" Angel asked.

"No. I'd heard from a relative of his before that he'd been trying to find me. I just didn't want to ruin my marriage. I'd already messed up once." Dorothy tightened her robe as if she'd been physically violated by thoughts of her past.

"That man you saw is Kevin." A lump filled her throat. She'd said his name in her head, but this was the first time in years that she said his name to anyone else. "Kevin and I met about a year before Anthony and I got together. We went on a few dates and really fell for each other." Dorothy's lips curled upward, and Angel noticed. She returned a smile to her. "We stopped talking shortly before I met Anthony. I was never quite sure why because it happened so abruptly."

The sun penetrated the glass, warming Dorothy's face and hands. She took a moment before she continued. She wanted to tell this story to someone for years and just so happened a teenager was willing to listen. Dorothy no longer cared about age, she just needed someone to hear her.

"Anthony and I got very serious a few months later and it helped me move on. About a year into dating Anthony, he proposed to me in April of '95 and we knew without any reservations that we were going to be together for a long time. My family was so excited."

Dorothy remembered the moment like it was yesterday. She remembered how he looked into her eyes, rubbing her cheek with his thumb when he proposed, his lips round and perfect. She released a short giggle. "He was just as handsome then as he is now."

Angel stared at Dorothy, catching each piece of the story one sentence at a time.

"He wanted to get married a few months after he proposed. So, we began planning the wedding. His presence pulled me away from Kevin. I felt like my king had arrived."

Suddenly, something crossed Dorothy's mind. She wanted to know what others would think of her if they discover the truth about her life. What will Maria say if Anthony tells Daniel his reason for leaving? What will Sharon say if she hears about Dorothy's infidelity, although it was long ago? And the Nortons? Dorothy had respect for them. They were the older ones in the community whose marriage was a great example to the younger couples. If they found out about this situation, she'd be embarrassed.

"A month before my wedding I ran into Kevin at a store. I can still remember how I felt when I saw him." She imagined the thick smell of cologne that traveled from his clothes, grasping her very soul like a chain yanking a parked car. "It was like I knew our relationship wasn't over, but I was getting married to someone else I loved. He told me this story about his mom being sick and he had to leave to be with her and his sisters in Colorado. I didn't believe him at first, but then the more he talked, the more I believed."

"Why did it still matter to you though? You met your king, right?" Dorothy was surprised by Angel's question.

"I think it mattered because I wanted it to matter. I thought our relationship was going to get stronger at one point, but then he just left. So, it mattered. I needed to know why. After seeing and talking to him, I just wanted to be with him again. A few days later we...," she paused. "You know we..." She couldn't bring herself to form those words to a teenager, but Angel knew exactly what she was saying. A tingle slithered down Dorothy's spine and goose bumps blossomed on her arms. She'd kept this inside for almost 19 years and now it was out. It felt like a ton lifted off her shoulders.

"I found out I was pregnant with Bobby a month after Anthony and I got married. At first, I did not think anything of it because Anthony and I tried to have a child as soon as we got married. He really wanted a son." Dorothy shrugged at her own comment. "Doctors went off my word to determine my due date. They asked when I had my last period, when did I start feeling sick and all that stuff. I answered those questions honestly. I went into labor a month before my due date. We were terrified." Panic infiltrated her voice when she said it. She thought about how she felt when she was about to lose Bobby during birth. She was so relieved to see his precious face looking toward her. She didn't lose him that day.

"The doctors were confident that he was fine. When he was born, he was healthy. He wasn't the size of a premature baby." She remembered holding Bobby in her arms. He was the best thing that ever happened to her. Dorothy rubbed his head, touched his little nose, and kissed his cheek. "He was seven pounds and eleven ounces. Just as healthy as any other baby."

Angel looked at the picture of Bobby that clung to the refrigerator, an apple magnet keeping it in place. Dorothy's eyes followed Angel's.

"As time went on, I could see the resemblance of Kevin appearing in him. Anthony always thought he resembled me."

"So where do you think Anthony went last night?" Angel interrupted Dorothy. Her eyes were fastened on her with curiosity.

Dorothy looked at the clock. He'd been gone for ten hours now. "I don't know. I hope he's okay." Angel reached over and placed her hand on Dorothy's.

All Angel could manage was, "I'm sure he is."

Anthony
April 12, 2014
Morning

Anthony took a deep breath when he awakened as if he'd been drowning. He hoped last night was a dream. He picked up the liquor bottle that rested on the nightstand half full. He glanced at the cheap, shabby curtains and knew that last night was real. Engines and horns wrapped around the atmosphere outside the motel. He sat on the edge of the bed and inhaled the smell of mothballs. The room began to spin as he tried to steady himself. He couldn't figure out how he landed in such a cheap motel when he could've stayed in any hotel he wanted. In his mind's eye he saw a man standing in front of him, telling him that Bobby was not his son. The thought of the thing made him sick. He couldn't envision Dorothy keeping such a secret from him.

Someone yelled outside and then there was a sudden burst of wild laughter, but it ceased abruptly. The television was on, but silenced. Orange, green, and blue squiggly lines waved across the screen, a comical rainbow. Anthony wobbled to the bathroom, holding his head and stomach. He felt awful. He needed to splash water on his face, but he wasn't sure what good it would do. He leaned on the sink and that's when he saw it. At first, he wondered how it got there. *Was someone else here with me last night? What did I do?* He splashed the water on his face and dried it with a white hand towel. He opened the towel and placed it flat in his hand, before turning his palm downward to pick up the gun. It was chrome and heavy. After close examination, he realized the gun was his.

He traipsed over to the bed, trying to remember what happened. He looked at the bottle and it was almost empty. The last time he drank like that was almost twenty years ago. His phone sang a jazzy tune and he reached in his pockets, but it wasn't there. It was on the bed close to the pillow. Dorothy's name flashed above a vibrant photo of her smiling, her hair Shirley Templed down her shoulders. He wasn't ready to talk to her. Instead of picking up the phone, he got undressed and went into the bathroom.

The shower felt good to his face. Thin slits of water raced down his stomach, rolling over the small strands of curled hair on his lower back. It was then that he remembered what happened. He panicked for a moment. *This can't be right. This can't be right. Did I really?* Questions swarmed his mind and rushed through his head like a movie, scene by scene.

HE'D BEEN SITTING in his car in an empty parking lot. The rain had finally come. It beat against his car, sounding like a thousand finger taps. The liquor bottle was on the passenger side, already half gone. Even while he was in the shower, he could feel himself pondering something, a deep question, a problem needing to be solved. The overwhelming feeling of Bobby not being his son hovered over him like a dark cloud. Then it hit him. *He is my son. He is my son,* he thought. He was the one who took care of Bobby. He was the one who taught him how to be a man. He clothed him and fed him. Wasn't that enough to qualify him as being the father.

Tears streamed down his face. All the things he did for Bobby and with Bobby had been snatched away too early. One thought led to another: the night in Dell Park, the money, the drug dealer and the man claiming to be Bobby's father. Anger filled his heart. How far would they go to get the money? And that's when the idea resurrected once again. Find the man who did this.

He allowed the water to drip down his face. His head thick with confusion. The memory came back again, within seconds. Anthony didn't want to think about it anymore, a flood of memories like a tsunami crashing to shore.

He had pulled onto a street, not remembering how he had gotten there. Anthony sat in front of a two story, modular home, two-car garage attached. The street was dark, and Ronnie was right, the house was pushed back into the woods. No other activity was taking place. It was only Anthony sitting alone in the dark. Time had gone by. Thoughts about Bobby swarmed his mind with pleasant memories. He missed him so much. At the moment he thought of Bobby, lights flashed quickly across the back glass of his car, but they drove past, never looking towards Anthony's car. A few minutes later he heard another engine. The engine calmed as it approached, pulling into the yard of the house he was watching.

The red brake lights flashed, followed by a quick blink of the parking lights, before a muscular man got out the car. He was not as tall as Anthony imagined. He was alone and that surprised Anthony for some reason. He took him to be a person who was always surrounded by someone for protection. Rage crawled into Anthony like an ugly, fierce animal. He wanted to kill him because someone should pay for Bobby's death. He grabbed his gun from under the seat and emerged from the car toward the house. The man stood to the garage door, pulling on something, struggling to open it. The garage door bounced up and down, making a popping noise. Anthony wondered what he was going to do when he reached him. So many things went through his mind like lightning bolts. He imagined asking him questions. He thought about punching him, but each time those thoughts came into his mind, it only circled back around to him killing the man. Anthony walked to the asphalt driveway. The moon was pitched high above their heads as if to light the way for Anthony. He reached the car and heard a faint cry, someone whining. A little girl.

What am I doing? He mumbled to himself. He remembered the quick jerk of the man turning towards him after hearing the noise from the car. He changed his mind and wanted to tuck the gun into the front of his pants. He just wanted to ask him some questions, but the man darted quickly towards him. Anthony was thrown onto the car and a blow connected with his right jaw. Anthony punched back, causing the man to stumble on the ground. The gun slipped from Anthony's hand and slid over the concrete. He could hear the little girl screaming from the car. "Stop, Daddy. Stop!" She cried. Anthony wanted to stop. He wanted to run to his car and leave, but he had to fight for his life. The man ran into Anthony again, jamming his back into the hood of the car. He leaned towards the ground and Anthony realized he was trying to get the gun. Anthony lifted his leg and kicked the man in the side. He tumbled over. Anthony released blow after blow to the man, but he just wanted to leave now. He regretted going there.

The man managed to make it to his feet after forcing himself from under Anthony, pushing him back a few inches. But Anthony had the gun in his hand now. The man pulled a blade from his pocket and charged Anthony. The little girl let out a threatening scream, then all went silent. Anthony heard nothing else, not even the pop that exploded from the weapon. The man slumped to ground, back against the car. Anthony looked at the little girl. Her face was round, eyes bulbous. Her hair was braided with little beads on each one. He felt like crying, he thought he should hug her. He ran to his car and drove away.

ANTHONY GOT OUT the shower, wiping the towel across his face, hoping to erase the memory.

Sharon
April 12, 2014
Morning

Sharon pulled her hair between her fingers, twisting it childishly. She looked out the window and Daniel's car was home. She imagined them arguing, her name being thrown around like paper in fire, increasing the flames. She wanted to say something to explain her actions, but there was nothing to say. She was a monster, kicking a woman while she was down.

She left her bedroom, her thoughts clouded with Daniel and all the wrong they'd done together. As she approached the kitchen, she saw Terrell. He stared at his toast, twisting and turning it. Placing it on the plate then resting his hand under his chin. She'd never seen him in such deep thought and all she could think of was how he lost two of his friends in one night.

"I was wondering when you were coming down." Terrell said when he noticed her.

Sharon peered around the corner, noticing Nicole wasn't in there.

"Is Nicole upstairs?"

"Yeah. She's awake though."

Sharon poured herself a glass of water and gulped it, cooling her throat, chest, and then belly.

"Did you hear me?" Terrell asked.

"I'm sorry, what is it?" She shook her head as if to get rid of the thoughts that were invading her mind.

"Do you want some toast?"

She didn't remember him asking the question.

"No. I'm not hungry"

Nicole came downstairs. Her hair bounced beautifully, and her clothes fit her so perfectly. In Sharon's eyes Nicole was perfect. Her teeth were aligned perfectly, her hair set in a ponytail, bun, or anything else perfectly, and she had the perfect face. Nicole gave Sharon a hug and Sharon kissed her forehead. There was something different about Nicole though. She didn't smile as much as she used to. Terrell noticed it, but Sharon did not. Sharon had become so consumed in Daniel that she lost her connection with Nicole. She always asked Terrell to look out for his sister while she did other things. Nicole released her hug and stood next to Terrell.

SHE WAS TOO embarrassed to stay there. She had a penchant for Daniel and didn't know how to get rid of those feelings. How could she look Maria in the face again? The door creaked as she pushed into her bedroom. Although the windows were opened, the curtains remained, no breeze, absolute stillness. She stood by the bed wanting to pick up her phone, dial Maria's number, and tell her how sorry she was. *I am sorry for ruining your marriage and life.* She imagined herself choking up as she apologized, but getting nothing but silence, a slam of the receiver with a long hum of the dial tone. Instead, she picked up the phone and called one of her friends. The phone rang once.

"Hello."

"Hey, Trish. It's me Sharon."

"Sharon, how are you?" She was excited to hear Sharon's voice. "Where have you been the past few months? I haven't heard anything from you?" Everything revolved around Daniel, someone else's husband. She couldn't respond truthfully.

All she managed was, "I've just been busy with life and these kids. You know how things can be."

Trish chuckled and agreed. "What's up? You need something?"

"As a matter of fact, I do. Would you happen to have any more houses for rent on your list?" Trish was one of the best realtors in town. They'd been buddies since college and when Trish moved nearby, Sharon introduced her to two more realtors, Daniel and Maria.

"Is this for you or someone else?"

"For me. I'm just looking around."

"Well I do have a few houses available. Is there anything in particular you're looking for?" Sharon was glad she didn't question her move. That's what she liked about Trish, business was business and friendship was friendship. She knew how to keep it separate.

"Just something simple for me and the kids. I'm not trying to move into anything too fancy and I'd like for it to be in the same school district."

"Give me one second to look at something." She paused. The clicking of computer buttons vibrated through the phone.

Sharon imagined her tapping each key with a pen in her mouth. She held a pen in her mouth all the time when she worked on important things.

"I just wanted to double check, but I have two in your school district. When do you want to see them?"

"Whenever you are free to do so, but I would like for it to be kind of soon."

"Why such a rush? Running away from something?" There was the friendly joke, but Sharon didn't know how to handle this one. She laughed it off without answering.

"I'm free to show you on Friday evening…say around five. Is that good for you?"

"Yes."

"Let me just make a note of it here." She lengthened each word verbally as she wrote them down. Meet. Sharon. On. Falls Road. "Okay, got it. See you then."

Maria
April 12, 2014
Morning

The glass slipped from her hand and crashed to the floor. She swept the little pieces from under the table as Daniel emerged from their bedroom. The glass clattered when she dropped the pieces into the empty trash can.

"Are you okay?" Those were the first three words he'd said to her since she caught him and Sharon together. The words rolled off his tongue as if he wanted to ask her the question all week and the timing was now perfect. She cut her eyes in his direction, never answering. She knew what Daniel thought and the question he really wanted to know the answer to, *Was she going to leave him?* Yes, that was her plan. There was no need for her to be with someone she couldn't trust during the most painful time in her life.

He folded his arms and leaned against the wall. She could feel him staring at her, but she didn't want to look back. He walked toward her and extended his hand, reaching for her shoulder. She snatched away.

"I just want to know are you okay, that's all." He acted like she had the flu, or a bad headache and he wanted to know if she was better.

"No!" she yelled. She wanted to say more, but she didn't know where to begin. "This marriage is over." She blurted the words out before she could think about it. "You have lied to me and I just don't know how I can forgive you." The words continued to pour out of her as if she'd practiced it. "You manipulated me with your lies and I just can't take it anymore. I cannot be with you without seeing how deceptive you are!" He smirked. It made her upset.

"You don't have anywhere else to go," he said with surety. "What are you going to do? Are you going to move back with your family?" His facial expression changed. He didn't seem as concerned as he was a minute ago. It was as if she was talking to a completely different Daniel.

"I'm not going anywhere, but you are."

He threw his head back like an evil villain and chuckled, "You can't put me out. I pay the mortgage here too. Who do you think you are?"

"I thought I was your wife," she said. "And there is something else too," she began. "I found out about your other insurance policy on Jason." Maria grabbed the papers from her purse and slammed them on the breakfast nook. There was nothing to hide any more.

"So, did you hire someone to kill our son? Did you plan for it to happen while we were in Florida, because it sure seems like a clever plan? It's ironic that he was murdered only two weeks after you had the policy changed."

"Let me explain," he pleaded.

"Explain what? Your lies?" She walked closer to him and without warning, slapped him across the face. She'd never hit Daniel before. She'd never hit anyone before hitting Sharon.

"Just listen for a second," he asked again. "Please-Please, just listen." He marched behind Maria in only his boxers and white tee-shirt. "Will you listen to me?" He managed to maneuver himself in front of her and grabbed her shoulders.

"Yes, I increased the policy because Jason was living reckless," he admitted.

"So, you needed to make more money from his reckless lifestyle. We already had a policy on him."

"I know what it…"

"And then you didn't tell me about it," she interrupted. "What were you planning to do with it? Skip town with Sharon and use the money for a new life with her." The thought infuriated her. "Just get your things and get out!"

He couldn't say another word. He knew there was no way to fix the mess he'd made. Wondering if she would call the police, he fumbled through his clothes and put on a pair of jeans and a shirt. She wondered if Daniel really got rid of their only child. Did she really believe that? He came from the bedroom with a bag in his hand. He paused in front of the breakfast nook and asked, "Are you sure you want to do this?"

And without a doubt she said, "Yes."

Angel
April 12, 2014
Morning

The dreams came again last night, too close together than previous times. This time I am lying on my back, not seeing anyone, but feeling the pressure of another being on me. I can feel the fear popping on my skin like goosebumps. Then Bobby runs over, as he did that night, and pushes the person to the ground. I awake from what little sleep I've gotten.

My thoughts switch from the dream to Anthony and his whereabouts, hoping he hasn't gotten hurt or anything. I know something else is going on with him on top of Bobby being murdered and now finding out he is not his father must be devastating. A chill goes down my spine as I stare at the white ceiling, ceiling fan spinning cool air. The guy in Dell Park said Anthony and Bobby were in the park at the same time on the night Anthony was attacked. Did Bobby know it was his father? I answer my own question. If he knew he would have returned the money.

I continue to stare at the ceiling. The longer I stare at it the more it looks like it is getting closer to me, possibly squeezing me between it and the bed. I hear Dorothy moving around. I take my eyes off the ceiling and look at the door. The vacuum is not running, but she bustles back and forth past the door, in a rush; hurried. I don't want to talk to her right now. There are too many things on my mind. Darla even crosses my mind once or twice this morning, but I push her out of it, hoping she hasn't reported me missing. Maybe she doesn't care because it was almost my birthday. She just never cared about me at all.

Dorothy walks by again. This time she stops right in front of the guest room. Maybe she's listening, trying to see if I'm awake. I remain still, I even try to hold my breath as if she can hear the air escape my lungs, but she moves past the door after a few seconds. The sun light shines through the small space between the hanging curtains. My eyes follow the thin strip of light that reaches across the carpet and lights the little black book. I thought I put it under my pillow last night, but maybe I didn't. Terrell shoots back into my thoughts. He didn't seem too interested in in the journal. Maybe there is nothing to this. Maybe I am blowing it out of proportion.

I want to see Terrell again, hear his affable voice. I try to think of a reason to go over, but nothing comes to mind. I open the journal unconsciously, flipping through pages, reading of murders. Why would someone write about this? I close the book and flip it from front to back a couple of times. I flip it to the back and there is a small inscription at the bottom. I sit onside the bed quickly and hold it closely to my face. The emblem is something I've seen before, black mamba.

I STAYED IN the room all day, except to use the bathroom. I am not ready to face Dorothy yet. I go to the bedroom window and see Daniel's car leaving the yard. My eyes scan the neighborhood from the guest room. No activity at the Norton's. Anthony's car is not here yet. Terrell's light is on. I want to go over to Terrell's to talk to him or Maria's to show her this journal. I decide to get dressed and go to Terrell's. My stomach growls and I realize I haven't eaten all day.

I pull open the bedroom door. The only sound comes from the television. Dorothy is nowhere in sight. I go to the bathroom and turn on the hot water to brush my teeth. The toothpaste buzzes in my mouth. I look at my teeth when I'm finished and rub my tongue across the top row; smooth, clean. I open the bathroom door and there is Dorothy, standing there. It creeps me out at first until I see she looks nervous, shook up. First, I say nothing, but she looks like she is going to collapse. She bursts into tears and walks past the bathroom and goes directly into her bedroom. I remain quiet. I don't know what to say to her that will make the pain of her mistake go away.

The moon hangs in the sky, bright orange, like a Chinese lamp. It's almost scary, hanging low in the sky as if it is going to drop in someone's front yard and roll towards me. The breeze brushes against my face. I imagine it wipes away the mark on my cheek, pushing it away like a feather into someone's yard, where the moon will be too. A light flicks off and a few minutes later, Sharon emerges from the front door. She comes out alone and gets into her car. At that moment I remember I left the journal upstairs. I run back up and there it is in the floor. I grab it and tuck it into my jacket like before and go back downstairs.

199

Sharon is gone. I sit down trying to figure out what to do next. Do I take this to Maria or Terrell? Maybe I should convince him there is more to this than what he thinks. I walk across the yard, feeling like I'm about to cross some unknown territory. The information that is in my jacket will shed new light on this whole incident. I can't figure out how all this is tied together, but maybe, just maybe, Daniel didn't have anything to do with Jason's murder. Maybe it was all a coincidence. Time seems to slow down as I move across the asphalt. I finally reach Terrell's yard, confusion hits the minute I reach it, but I don't know why. The closer I get, the more I feel I need to tell him.

The dew from the night grass crystalizes my shoes, making them look oddly appealing as I take each step. I walk around the back of the house this time. I look down and notice the basketball just moments before tripping over it. I am so glad Terrell was not out here to see the embarrassing stumble. I kick the ball to the side with my foot and it rolls only a short distance. I knock on the glass of the back door, but no one comes. I knock again and still no one. I leave the back porch and make a right to go to the front door and someone startles me. A shrill rumbles from my throat. I grab my chest and try to get my short rapid breaths back under control.

"You scared me." I say. It comes out before I realize it doesn't make sense for this person to be here this time of night.

"Why would I scare you?" Mr. Norton says. He leers at me, eyes downward, lips tight.

"What are you doing over here?" He doesn't answer. "Excuse me, I'm trying to go to the front door," I say trying not to sound scared. I try to pass him, but he grabs my arm. "Let go of me."

"Where's my journal?" His narrowed eyes gaze into mine.

How could he possibly know I had a journal? I didn't tell anyone except Terrell and then the unthinkable crosses my mind. Did Terrell tell him about the journal?

"I don't have your journal," I struggle to say, trying to get him to release me.

"That's a lie. Give it to me now." He presses into my stomach and touches the hard object. I try to run, but he catches me by the hood of my jacket, jerking me down to the ground, causing me to hit my head. He pulls me by my hood, then his hand moves to my hair and he drags me to his house. I try to fight to get away, but the pressure from my head injury slows me down. I kick my feet, but he is much stronger than I thought. A scream squeezes from my vocal cords, but it doesn't seem loud enough. He puts his hands under my arms and lifts me slightly, but still pulling me. I realize he's dragged me to his house. A short lady that I've never seen before stands on the back step with the mouth of the house waiting to swallow me. Then my head slams against the floor. All goes black.

Sharon
April 12, 2014
Late Night

Sharon shoved her keys into the front door and wriggled it until the door finally unlocked. Late nights like this would usually include Daniel, but not this time. The house was quiet, except the small chatter coming from the television. Sharon walked upstairs, gently massaging her sore muscles. She turned her neck from side to side, feeling the pain hit her shoulders. She imagined herself tumbling off the bed and onto the floor with Maria in her arms. She was embarrassed at the thought.

Her bedroom door was ajar. The silhouette of a dark figure caught her attention. She pushed the door open gently and there was Nicole, stretched wildly across her bed with only the night light on. She smiled, thinking of how much time she was going to regain by focusing on her family. The more time she focused on Daniel, the less time she focused on Nicole and Terrell. She closed the door and went into the bathroom.

THE WATER WARMED her skin. She relaxed her back and closed her eyes, placing the warm cloth over her face. Although she didn't want to think about Daniel, various images came to her mind. Her and Daniel at the cabin a few months ago. They had dinner that night and nothing else. Another image came. They were at the movies. It was raining that night. She caught herself smiling as she thought about it. He had his arms around her shoulder; the umbrella perched above their heads, laughing as they ran to the car. *How dangerous? How stupid? How awkwardly fun!* She thought.

The bath gave the opposite effect of what she desired. She wanted to relax, calm her mind, instead it wandered uncontrollably, one thought leading to the next like wrong turns being made repeatedly, never coming out at the right spot. She pushed the release knob and the water bellowed as it tornadoed down the drain. She remained in the tub and the water receded from her chin, reaching her shoulders, then breast, and finally her stomach.

She dressed in pink and red Mickey Mouse pajamas and went into Nicole's bedroom to be alone for a little while. Nicole's room smelled of coconut shampoo and bubble gum. Textbooks were stacked neatly on her bureau; Science, English, and History. Two stuffed bears gazed at Sharon from the bed, as if they both knew her secret and the secrets of others. She sat on the bed and without hesitation bounced back to her feet as if she sat on pins and needles. She needed to pack some clothes for them, send them to their father's, just until she moved.

After searching for some things in the closet, she went to the dresser. A picture of Bobby greeted her. She became angered, not by the picture, but by her selfishness. How could she have been so wrapped in herself that she hadn't been to visit Dorothy after the funeral? She flipped the picture over and read, **To: Nicole, From: Bobby** and placed it back how she found it.

Sharon pulled Nicole's suitcase toward her bed. It was light, unused. She unzipped it and began to look through the clothes in her dresser to pack some things, opening the top drawer and slamming the clothes into the suitcase. She opened the second drawer and did the same, finally reaching the third drawer and removing all her clothes, putting them angrily into the suitcase as if Nicole had done something wrong. Before she closed the drawer, she noticed something. It was a diary she had purchased for Nicole last year. She took it out and flipped through the pages, expecting to see nothing but empty sheets. Instead, it was the opposite. The pages weren't empty, but very full. Before she realized what she was doing, she began reading it.

Terrell
April 12, 2014
Late Night

I am always thinking about different things, things that don't make sense sometimes. What would happen if I died? Where would I go? Is there life after life? These questions rage through my mind like a strong current, pulling and pushing thoughts whichever way it pleases.

The house is quiet. There is no one to talk to and I wish Angel was here. Mom is always busy, and Nicole is always isolated, but I understand why. Our lives have changed dramatically over the past few weeks. At least some sense of normalcy has tried to return since Angel has come here. Her face is beautiful. I feel like I owe her something since Bobby was her best friend.

I stare at the television before I feel like I am drifting into a deep sleep, but I fight it. I go into the kitchen and grab a soda. The moon light shines directly into the kitchen, illuminating the table and wall directly behind it.

I pour a glass of orange juice and go back into the living room, thinking those thoughts again. I lay back on the couch and I hear a little bit of movement upstairs.

It is 11:34 p.m. and Mom still isn't home. Suddenly, I hear a tap. I don't get up right away. I assume it is Nicole doing something upstairs. I hear another tap and this time I sit straight up. It comes again but followed by two people talking outside. I get a little nervous. Not scared, only nervous. A faint scream hits me. I jump to my feet and go to the side window. I see something that shocks and enrages me. It is Mr. Norton pulling Angel across the yard by her hoodie or hair, I can't tell. I put on my shoes and shirt, creep out the back door, head to the Norton's. I see a flash of light swipe alongside the house and it is Mom. She pulls into the driveway as I run from our house to Mr. Norton's.

Bobby
February 16, 2014
Evening

When Jason said it, Bobby sat straight up. Jason was leaned back comfortably on the hood playing a game on his phone.

Bobby stared at him for a moment. Jason finally looked at him before taking the final sip of his beer. Jason threw the can to the ground, crushing it under his foot. Bobby sat on the hood of his mom's car and Jason leaned on the driver's side door. His face was austere and stoic. No apologetic look or unsureness from his comment.

A few people straggled around Dell Park. An old man with a long, dirty brown coat that reached his calf was bent over by a tree, picking up grass then letting it fall feather-like to the ground.

"Are you crazy?" Bobby finally said. Jason looked and shook his, but not answering the question.

"What would you do if this was your father? What would you do to someone who hurt your mother?" The question hit Bobby like a ton of bricks. He never put himself in Jason's shoes since Jason discovered the issue. Anger slithered into Bobby. That was the key question that convinced him. He didn't fully agree to the plan, but the seed had been planted.

"This is not cool."

"And what Sharon has done isn't cool either. She walks around this neighborhood like she is put together so well, but then she's nothing but a..." he let Bobby fill in the blank with whatever word he saw fit. Bobby listened to the words as they came between gritted teeth.

"If she did this to my mom, she will do it to your mom." Everything around Bobby silenced. Jason was right.

"But that's Terrell's family."

"What do I care?" He turned quickly toward Bobby; spittle hit the hood of the car and another landed on his own bottom lip. Bobby thought of Nicole. She wasn't that kind of girl. She wasn't like her mother.

"Whether you're in or not, I'm going to teach her a lesson. She doesn't want to mess with me." Jason proclaimed. Bobby guzzled the last bit of beer in his can. He tossed it into the trash can that was only a few feet away from the car. He found himself staring at the sky after Jason got quiet, imagining those innocent waves from Sharon to his dad, now becoming flirtatious waves. Bobby pictured her leaning on Anthony's shoulder, laughing and giving him girlish hits on the arm, while Dorothy was in the kitchen, laughing about the joke from a distance. He got angry instantly.

If she's ruined Jason's family, she'll do the same to mine.

March 3, 2014

BOBBY THOUGHT ABOUT the things Jason asked of him. He wouldn't let up off it, constantly beating it into Bobby's head for the past two weeks. He wanted to do it last week, but that wouldn't have worked. The timing wasn't right. It rained. It snowed. Dorothy wasn't feeling well so Bobby had to help her. Then he noticed increased questioning from Anthony. "Have you seen anyone come into the neighborhood you don't recognize?" Bobby answered him truthfully, but he still asked throughout the week. Bobby watched him peak out of windows, checking his phone, and looking over his shoulders before he went to work.

Bobby crossed the street to meet Jason. Jason wore his blue polo shirt, jean shorts, and black boots. He stood outside on the lawn and before Bobby's feet touched the dewy grass, he announced that his parents were gone for the weekend; Maria visited her parents in North Carolina, Daniel had gone to Pennsylvania on a business trip. He mentioned they would be in Florida at the end of the month on another business trip.

They went into the house and Jason stood over the vent, allowing the heat to brush up his shorts and rounding his shirt at the waist. He moved suddenly from the vent and walked to the bathroom with a sudden burst of energy. He came back with a collection of pills in his hand.

"What's that?"

"What I told you about. It will put her right to sleep."

Bobby didn't respond. He couldn't believe he was having this conversation about Nicole. Jason handed Bobby a rolled blunt and two cans of beer. He lit the blunt, inhaling the weed deeply into his lungs, feeling his head buzz. Then exhaled.

"Text her now. Tell her we are here by ourselves."

Bobby did just that.

WYD

Watchin t.v like always. WBU

"What did she say," Jason asked.

Bobby didn't respond.

Over Jason's house. U want 2 come over?

Yeah.

Is your mom there? Is Terrell awake?

No. She went out of town and he is asleep. I'll be over.

Jason stood quietly as the text messages went back and forth. Bobby discerned Jason's impatience. Jason dumped the pills on the table, counted them, and then scooped them back into his palm, candy-like.

They watched her run across the backyard and come to the house. Jason opened the door, letting her in. Nicole was dressed in a hooded sweatshirt, blue jeans, and some winter boots. She pulled the hood off her head and her hair dropped to her shoulders.

"So, what y'all up to tonight?"

Jason turned his back when she asked the question, leaving Bobby to make up something. "Nothing. Just trying to find something to do." She put her sweatshirt on the rack and peaked around the corner into the living room.

The lights were dimmed, the curtains glowed around the light, and the glass vases seem crystalized. Bobby felt dirty. He knew what was about to happen. His stomach felt like it was turning inside out. He almost felt sorry for her because it wasn't her fault, but then he thought about those constant words that Jason had been saying for the past few weeks. They rung in his ears even louder than before. She opened her mouth to speak, but Jason interrupted.

"Here's something to drink."

He gave them both a glass and walked back into the kitchen. Bobby imagined Jason tossing the pills back and forth between his hands before dropping them slowly into the glass.

"I'll be right back," Bobby said.

Jason wasn't in the kitchen. Bobby sauntered down the hall into the bathroom, but he wasn't there either. He went in Maria's room and there was Jason, standing to the window.

"What are you doing?"

"Just thinking. I'm coming out." He looked over his shoulder in Bobby's direction but didn't give him full attention.

"How soon before the pills work? I mean did you put the pills in the drink?"

"No. I changed my mind. I want her to know what's going on." He put his hands into his pockets as if he was some psychologist telling Bobby how to handle a patient. His face vulpine.

When Bobby went to Nicole her face was calm, relaxed. She smelled of coconut. Bobby imagined her rubbing herself down in sweet smelling lotion before coming over. "So how long are you going to be over here?"

He stretched mechanically and yawned. "I'm staying the night. My parents don't mind."

Jason came into the living room as soon as Bobby finished his sentence. He glared at them. His eyes looked full of rage, but Nicole wasn't looking at Jason, she looked directly at Bobby as if there was something she wanted to say. She smiled. Her cheeks moved closer to her eyes. Her white teeth were set perfectly, and Bobby admired them briefly. He wondered what she was going to say. *Does she want me to be her boyfriend? Is she going to compliment me?*

Suddenly the room went dark, darker than Dell Park after midnight. Daniel and Maria's picture clattered to the floor, cracking the gold frame. Nicole screamed.

"Shut up." He wanted to put his hand over her mouth, but he couldn't.

The smallest sounds seemed equally loud to her yelling. Her body moved back and forth. She tried to set her hands free, but Bobby held them tighter. She cried and then her screams turned into a small whimper. She wondered why this was happening and turned her head to look at Bobby as he held her arms above her head, but she couldn't see anything. She wished she'd stayed home, repentantly.

Jason pressed a hard fist in her chin as she squirmed away. "Don't you tell anyone about this, or I will kill you. Do you hear me?" His face was red, hair sweaty. Nicole crawled into the kitchen, jeans in her hands. A trail of tears followed her. She put on her pants quickly, grabbed her hooded sweatshirt without putting it on, and ran home.

Jason zipped his pants. Bobby threw himself back on the couch, never turning the light back on. He gazed at the dark ceiling, wondering how he allowed himself to do such a hideous thing. He rued the day.

Jason walked outside toward the pond. He stepped over small sticks, puddles of water, and a branch to get to the pond. The crickets screamed loudly, and the frogs shouted over them. Jason gazed at the water, with nothing on his mind. He just wanted to go outside. There was no guilt in his heart. No remorse for what he'd done. He felt himself sinking. He stood in muddy waters, mud gripping to the sole of his boots.

"Dang!" He yelled as he looked down at his boots. He went inside the house and took off his boots by the kitchen door, never putting them on again, mud hardening around the soles. He went into the living room to talk to Bobby, but Bobby had gone home to his parents.

Angel
April 13, 2014
Early Midnight

I'm at Mama Wesley's. I never thought the time would come again where I'd see them. The day seems all too familiar and lucid. It's late at night. I am the only one awake. Mama Wesley rests on her bed while I watch television downstairs. Suddenly, there's a knock at the front door. I go to answer it and it's her grandson. He is older than me and most of the kids in the neighborhood, eighteen years old.

"Where is Ma-Ma?" He asks.

"She's asleep," I say as he peers over my shoulders as if I am lying.

"So, what you doing?"

"Just watching this movie. I've never seen the clown movie, "It."

"It's not all that scary." He walks to the couch and plops down.

I don't feel right about him being here.

"Come sit beside me," he demands.

I do.

He puts his hand on my thigh. I move his hand away.

"Don't you want me?"

"No."

I stand to my feet, heading to the front door to make him leave. He follows me, but instead of walking past me, he pushes me outside with him, wrestling me to the side of the house, covering my mouth. He forces me to the ground and makes me have sex with him. Then I see someone. I see Bobby, the kiddish Bobby. He pushes the boy off me, hits him and her grandson runs away. I don't think he was afraid of Bobby, merely didn't want to get caught.

I explain to Mama Wesley what happened the next morning, but he beat me to it. Saying I coaxed him into having sex with me and when Bobby caught us, I was too embarrassed, so I made up a story about him raping me. They don't believe me; they believe him. Next thing I know Mama Wesley cuts my long, thick hair. She said I thought I was too cute because of it and that's why I wanted to sleep with him. They plan to have me removed from the best home I've ever had.

I AWAKE TO rapid breathing. I am confused as to whose breathing it is until I suddenly realize it is my own. I try to catch my breath, then I begin to reach into my pocket to get my asthma pump. Some force prohibits me. It has not registered yet as to what is happening. Mr. Norton holds my hands down and I want to tell him to let me get my pump, but I choke on the words. Mrs. Norton locks the door. She slides an object across the floor and I only hear liquid being poured, splashing at the bottom, and then quieting as it rises. I try to retain minutiae of what's happening around me. I tell myself to calm down, catch my breath, or I will die in the hands of these people.

He drags me into the hall, placing me in a chair and fastening my hands around the back of it. The claustrophobic walls seem to close in on me. The hall is dark, but I can see shiny images glisten across the wall, a spark of glow here and spark of light there. The walls are decorated with beautiful frames, but I cannot see the faces that are hidden in them. The thick smell of bleach burns my eyes and sits on my tongue. I want to rub them, but I can't, so I close them tightly, then open them again, doing it repeatedly until I feel some relief. Suddenly I recognize where the smell comes from. Mrs. Norton is on her knees scrubbing something from the floor. She pours more bleach and scrubs again. Something wet drips down my face and runs down my cheek, reaching my lips. The metallic taste of blood rests on my tongue. She finally gets up and I realize I must've bled on her tiled kitchen floor. Mr. Norton walks into the other room and they begin to chatter, but I cannot understand what they are saying. I twist my hands to loosen it, but nothing happens. My feet are tied as well. He must hear my movements because he comes around the corner quickly and stares at me. "So, it was you who did this?" I manage. All I can envision is Mr. Norton pointing a gun towards my friend and pulling the trigger.

"Who do you think you are? You come into my neighborhood and take what belongs to me." The room spins as the words come out. *I didn't know it was yours.* The words form around my tongue, but melts like a bitter pill. My head hangs as I still work to regain control of my breathing. I try to block out the dark area that surrounds me so I can think rationally, but I'm unsuccessful. The darkness confuses me, frightens me. Mr. Norton's silhouette stands in front of me, the moon light outlining his figure. I close my eyes.

"How much do you know?"

"Nothing," I mumble.

"You lie!" He yells. I think of all the things I've read in his journal. I know what he's capable of; he is capable of murder.

"Honestly, I know nothing," I groan through the sharp pain in my head. I remember falling to the ground, hitting my head on something hard. *He doesn't believe me.* Another shape comes in front of the moon light. It is shorter and slightly thicker. Mrs. Norton. She slithers behind him but doesn't say anything.

"You have your journal now. Just let me go," I say.

He gives a villainy laugh and asks, "Do you think I'm stupid? You may still report me to someone. I can't have that."

"So, what are you going to do? Kill me?" I say it as if it is not an option. He must let me go. He cannot keep me forever. He doesn't respond to my question. He only chuckles, which causes my stomach to twist in knots. I know now he plans to kill me. He has no choice.

"I promise I won't tell anyone about what has happened. Just please let me go." I think of the nonrelatives I have to not think about me. They will go on about their normal lives not knowing what has happened. Mr. Norton and his wife go into a back room. Something drops to the floor. Then I hear a door opening and slamming into something. I imagine it is an underground door, but I don't know. They are talking, but their voices begin to fade, getting further and further away. I twist and turn my wrists again, but nothing happens. I drop my head, giving up at the task, accepting that I have gone too far. I should have never come to Beautiful Lane. The people here are just as reckless and careless as the people in the old neighborhood where I first met Bobby. They are just as crazy as Darla except they hide behind their beautiful suburban town.

Footsteps move toward me. I close my eyes and a shadow fall upon me. My space gets a little darker. My space feels a little warmer. I don't want to know how I am going to die so I keep my eyes closed. A familiar smell lingers under my nostrils. A warm hand grabs my arm and I open my eyes. It's Terrell.

He reaches behind my back to untangle the belt from my hands. I want to ask him how he knew, but he whispers for me to be quiet before I can utter a word. The belt drops from my hands and my arms feel heavy. My shoulders, sore. I undo my own feet and he grabs my hand.

Mr. Norton and his wife comes closer. Their voices travel down the dark hall. Mystified. Terrell holds my hand as we creep towards the back door and at that moment, I find solace in feeling his hands. The sweet smell of his skin floats into my nostrils. I think of his soft lips touching mine. Before we reach the door, I realize Mr. Norton is no longer speaking. The silence within the house terrifies me, even as Terrell stands here. We approach the door and he twists the doorknob, trying to prevent it from squeaking. Suddenly I am yanked backwards. It catches me off guard. I am thrown to the floor by Mr. Norton. Terrell turns around and pushes Mr. Norton backwards, causing him to stumble over a chair and fall to the floor. He gets up quickly and I remember the things I have read about him. I remember seeing him exercise every morning. This is not the average older man. He lunges into Terrell slamming his back against the counter and tossing him into the refrigerator. Terrell falls to the floor. I stagger back to my feet, feeling the throbbing of a headache. Mr. Norton begins to march towards Terrell, but he sees me recovering. He grabs my hair and pulls me into the living room. I catch sight of Mrs. Norton, who only watches the incident unfold. I try to plead to her for help, but she says nothing. He pushes me down on the couch.

"You're going to pay for what you've seen," he yells.

"You have the journal now. What else do you want? Just leave me alone!" I yell back.

He limps back into the kitchen and I hear a sudden sound of air getting caught in someone's throat. I stumble to the kitchen, head still foggy, and Terrell stands over Mr. Norton with a wooden object in his hand. Mrs. Norton looks as if she wants to lunge into Terrell, but she eyes the object in his hand. She kneels over her husband and pleads for him to get up. These are the first words I clearly understand coming from her. Terrell grabs my hand again, opens the back door, and we make a run towards his house. The journal is left behind. Mr. Norton has everything he wanted except my life, and I know I must get out of this town as soon as possible, or he may still take it.

Darla
April 13, 2014
Afternoon

It has been pure chaos around here since Angel decided she wanted to run away from home. You can provide a decent place for a person to live and they will still take advantage of you. She's lucky I even allowed her to stay here and then she goes and does something like this. I barely have anyone to watch after the twins now when we aren't home. I had no idea she was gone until Dan told me he was waiting to use the bathroom and he realized it was taking her too long. He said he knocked on the door several times, but she did not answer him. He heard the window being forced open and he kept calling her name, but she still didn't answer. Dan tried to force his way in there, which explains why the panel was cracked along the door's frame. He caught her climbing out the window and he tried to grab her, but it was too late.

The social worker came the next day and I just didn't know what to say. I wanted to tell the truth, but Dan said I should lie. He said we would find her, even if it was after her 18th birthday.

"Tell them she is with a friend and you gave her permission to get a break from the kids. They will understand that." He rubbed my shoulders as he talked as if what he was saying was the truth. "We don't want anything happening with the money you get, do we?" He was right. Ever since I'd taken her in, the income has helped me have extra money in my pocket and Dan has benefited from the money too, being that he hasn't had a job in a year now.

I sit in on my red chair, wondering where in the world she could have gone.

"When is Angel coming back?" I turn around and Kassey leans on the chair arm.

"I don't know when she is coming back, baby. We will find her okay."

"Have you called the cops? What if something happened to her?"

I pull Kassey closer to me and rub her head gently. She is so innocent. I don't have favorite kids, but Kassey is special to me. She is quiet, always wanting to explore new things. Her skin is pale because she barely goes outside during the day, only the evening. I rub my fingers across her pale arm and kiss her cheek.

"She is probably okay. I think she was upset, that's all."

"About what?" Kassey always wants an answer. Nothing can get by her.

"I don't know darling. Now go take a shower." I pat her on the shoulder, and she moves past me. I hear her walking down the hall, but her steps stop and then her footsteps get a little closer to me again. She pops around the corner as if she has something new to share.

"Mom, do you think Angel went to visit her dead friend?"

"What are you talking about?"

"Her friend died a couple of weeks ago. I was going to tell you, but I didn't think it was important. His name was Bobby."

221

I sit on the edge of my chair, feeling Kassey has just helped me, but I am unsure. "What do you know about Bobby?"

Kassey twirls the end of her hair as she talks. "I remember her going on The Book and finding out he was dead. She threw her phone down on the chair and ran into her bedroom and locked herself in there. I picked up her phone and knocked on the door to give it to her, but she wouldn't open it for me. I looked at it and saw all the stuff she had seen. His name was Bobby....Bobby." She looked at the ceiling as she tried to pull his last name from the air. "Bobby McKinley."

"Do you know when he died?"

"No, but it was only a few days before she left. You can probably go on The Book and check out his page."

After she says this, I tell her to get in the shower and I immediately log in The Book and search his name. There he is, his big, brown face as the cover photo. I look at his timeline and it is filled with "miss you" messages. I click on the "About" button and there is his address.

Dan comes storming out the bathroom.

"Why did you tell her to come in if you knew I was in there?" He says with anger.

I ignore the question. "I think I know where she is." I turn the phone toward him and point to Bobby's picture. "I think she went to this boy's house. His address is right here."

He takes the phone and examines it as if he knows the young man. He smiles and hands it back to me. He adjusts his pants and says, "Let's leave in the morning."

Anthony
April 13, 2014
Morning

The last few days had been a blur. He was nervous, paranoid, and suspicious of things around him. He was a murderer and there was no other way to look at it. The cause was justified, but it didn't make him different from any other murderer out there. He could still see the little girl's face, wet with tears as he ran away from the car. Yes, he wanted to stop. He changed his mind, but it was too late. The sudden flash of gunfire occurred to him again, the man falling to the ground, and the grievous look in his eyes as he sank low beside his car.

His car hummed; the steering wheel reverberated under his fingertips as he sat in his driveway on Beautiful Lane. Anthony didn't know where else to go. He imagined Dorothy standing to the kitchen counter, gazing out at the front lawn, greeted by roses and magnolias, as he wrapped his arms around her waist, kissing her neck. He exhaled and pushed open the car door.

The house was quiet. He peeked into the sunroom and no one was there. Anthony carefully walked up the steps, noticing the pictures of Bobby leading him upstairs; he stared at each photo, memories dangling from his mind like a man hanging from a cliff. He didn't want to let go, but if he held on, the pain would be unbearable.

The peaceful comfort of his bedroom welcomed him. The carpet felt softer. The room smelled sweeter. The walls seemed whiter and the bed looked more comfortable. Dorothy was in the bathroom and he heard the water rain into the tub from the showerhead.

The nozzle squeaked. He imagined the water sliding down her body, down her legs, and onto the tiled floor. The door pushed open. Anthony stared at her. One hand moved gently over her wet hair as she wrapped a white towel over her head. She gasped when she noticed him sitting on the bed. He stood to his feet and walked toward Dorothy. She looked down at the floor. He could feel the embarrassment for her. She stepped onto the carpet, leaving a trail of wet footprints behind.

He grabbed her hand gently. Her skin felt so soft.

"I miss you."

"I miss you, too," she said as the corners of her lips curled upward.

"I don't want to be without you. I don't want to lose you." He rubbed his thumb gently across the back of her hand.

"I am so sorry for what I've done, Anthony. I never meant to hurt you and I certainly didn't want it to come out like this," she said plaintive.

He didn't want her to explain herself anymore. He just wanted it to be over for them both, past mistakes left in the past. He pulled her closer to him, laying her head on his shoulders. He knew the importance of forgiveness now. He had to forgive her because there was someone out there now who will have to forgive him one day.

Dorothy lifted her head and looked into his eyes. They were brown and pleasant, comforting. Her lips connected with his and at that moment they felt like everything would be fine.

"I miss Bobby so much." The words came from Anthony's mouth with conviction.

"I do too. I miss him so much, Anthony. Why'd someone have to do this to us?" She stared into Anthony's eyes and a tear streamed down her face.

"Don't worry. Things will get better. He will always be a part of us."

"Kevin didn't even know Bobby was killed. He was coming to meet him." The name made Anthony uneasy. He didn't want his name coming from her mouth. The statement didn't matter anymore. He didn't raise Bobby, Anthony did.

"I just want you to know I love you. I will never leave you." He kissed her forehead. She looked at him and pushed him closer to the bed, climbing on him, continuing to kiss his lips and face.

"Where's Angel?"

"In. The. Guest. Room." Dorothy said between each kiss.

"No, she isn't. I thought she went back home." She stopped kissing him for a moment and he regretted bringing up Angel's name.

"No, she hasn't gone anywhere. She was just here last night. Dorothy went into the room and yelled back to him, "It looks like she didn't even stay here last night."

"Where do you think she is then?"

"She may be over Maria's or Terrell's. I saw her walking over there a few times."

The front door slammed.

"That must be her," Dorothy said. "Let me see if everything is fine."

Sharon
April 13, 2014
Morning

She didn't get much sleep last night after reading Nicole's diary. The contents were puzzling. She couldn't believe the secrets she held in her hands, a spilling of dark secrets on a beautiful street. Sharon had been so wrapped in her own life and someone else's husband that she missed the cry from her children when they needed her the most. Misery filled her stomach like steel dropping to the bottom of the ocean, landing hard in vast darkness, no one around to remove it. Bile formed in her throat, but she pushed it back down.

She gazed out the window and saw her neighbors living normally. In her eyes the Norton's were safe in their homes. She saw Anthony's car parked in the yard and admired him and Dorothy for a minute. They were loving, supportive of each other. That's all Sharon ever wanted. She imagined them sitting at the table drinking coffee, eating breakfast, and watching a favorite morning show. Sharon saw past the fact that their son had been murdered.

The diary was tight in her hands. The secrets it contained could not be revealed. *I must protect my children*, she thought. After all, it was her fault. She wasn't there for them.

A female voice was downstairs, but it didn't sound like Nicole's. There was another sound, but Sharon was too busy worrying about the diary that she didn't have the energy to search out the noise. She lifted the diary to her face and opened it again. The information was too heavy for her to accept as a mother, her heart was crushed. She wished the words were different. She wished it was full of things about girls Nicole hated, or friends she found out were not really her friends, but it was much heavier than that.

June 2, 2013

Today was a good day. Momma did my hair in this really cool style that I have been wanting for a long time. I guess she found time to do it for me. She's always busy. I cleaned my room and changed some things around. My television was in the way of opening my closet door all the way, so I moved that into another corner. Terrell went out to play basketball with some friends, so it was really quiet in here. I did not have to argue with him for the phone so that was good.

Sharon looked at the journal entry date and saw it was written several months ago.

June 7, 2013

It is the last day of school and I am so excited. We are going to have so much fun this summer. Momma said we all are going up to our dad's for a few weeks and she is coming with us. I hope they get back together. I think they secretly love each other. This boy told me today he liked me, but I'm only fourteen and Momma is not having any boys around anytime soon. He was cute though, but nahhh! Terrell had a girlfriend when he was fourteen, but Momma didn't know. He kissed that girl behind the school. I threatened him and told him to give me five dollars or else I would tell and he gave it to me.

Sharon remembered telling Nicole that she would be with them when they visited their father. She hoped they would get back together too, but things with Daniel had taken her attention away from him. She laughed at the thought of Terrell kissing some girl, although she didn't want her little girl to kiss someone behind a school building. She thought about their father again and she missed him. She flipped through a few pages, searching for that dreadful entry that she'd read last night.

March 4, 2014

Last night was the worst night of my life. I knew I was not supposed to talk to those boys, but I have known them for a long time. They have been friends with Terrell and I can't believe what they did. All I wanted to do was hang out with them because they told me I could. I thought Bobby liked me. He wanted me to come over, but he changed into a different person last night. When I got over there I regretted it. Jason and Bobby pulled me into one of the rooms and ripped my clothes off and made me have sex with Jason. I screamed, but it seemed like no one heard me. My heart is broken. I do not know how to tell anyone about this. This diary is the only thing I have right now. Momma is not here most nights. I don't know where she goes. All I can do is cry. I feel like killing myself. This is all my fault. I should have never gone over there.

Sharon was in disbelief all over again.

March 10, 2014

Terrell has been asking what is wrong with me. I was afraid to tell him because I know he likes to protect us. He is "the man of the house." I finally told him what happened and he was furious. I have never seen him that angry before. For some reason he asked me not to go to the police. He said he could handle it on his own. I asked him how, but he wouldn't answer. He only went into his bedroom and showed me a gun. I asked him where did he get it from, but he wouldn't tell me. He said he had it for protection being that he was the man of the house. I kept asking him what was he going to do, but he never answered me.

March 28, 2014

Jason and Bobby are dead and I am afraid. I do not want Terrell to get into trouble. He was only protecting me. I should've gone to the cops even though he told me not to. I did not know he loved me, his little ol'sister, that much. I will never be able to show him how much I am grateful for him. I am sorry they lost their lives, but why did they choose me. I look at Terrell every day, knowing that he's killed someone. He hasn't admitted it to me, but I know he did it. I could tell he was going to do something leading up to last night. He was angry all yesterday. He kept asking if I was okay. When I came downstairs he wasn't there. He came home about thirty minutes after I realized he was gone. I wish Mom was here. I know he did something. I could see it in his eyes when he came back home.

Sharon slammed the diary shut. How did she miss the pain in her daughter's eyes? How did she miss the hurt in Terrell? The reason behind Nicole's sudden isolation and shyness all made sense now.

"I've got to protect my children," she mumbled. Someone took her child's innocence and her son took someone's life. She thought about Dorothy and how much she loved her son. They always did things to support their kids, keeping them on the right track. Then she thought about Maria and Daniel. Daniel would hate her if he knew her son killed their child.

More noise surfaced downstairs. It was even louder than before, but this time it scared Sharon.

"Terrell?" She called out to him.

He didn't answer.

"Terrell?" She said again, "Is everything okay?"

"Yeah!"

She held the diary tightly to her chest and looked out the window again, but this time she saw something strange. It was Angel running across the street. For some reason she didn't look like she was running to something, but from something. She looked terrified.

Angel
April 13, 2014
Morning

My hand is placed on Terrell's leg and he places his hand on mine. He looks directly into my eyes and asks, "Are you okay?"

He wants to make sure that I am not hurt, although he asked me the same question last night after he rescued me from the Norton's. He brought me back to his house and neither of us said anything to each other, only sat in darkness before falling asleep on the couch.

I awake to him rubbing my hair and staring at me. The flat-screen television above the fireplace is on, but silenced. The neat area looks like no one ever does anything in here.

"Yes, I'm okay."

"Are you sure?" He asks.

"Yes."

He looks nervous, but brave. His eyes are directly on me and I sense the connection between us. The smell of his golden, brown skin attracts me to him, but I am nervous, still shaken up by what occurred just hours ago.

"Why did this happen? What is this about?" He asks. I can't believe he didn't ask sooner, but he was more concerned about me.

"Remember the journal I showed you," I begin. "It belongs to Mr. Norton. He is the one who murdered those people we read about. He knew Bobby and Jason found the book and he killed them."

He looks at me as if he doesn't believe me, but I continue to talk, trying to convince him of what I've discovered. He is puzzled. His thick skin wrinkles on his forehead. I believe he is surprised by my discovery.

"This is the reason why he attacked me. He knew I had the journal some kind of way and he wanted it back." He stares at me. "He specifically asked for his journal," putting emphasis on each word.

He still doesn't say anything. He removes his hand from mine and places my hand on my own leg. He stands to his feet and walks to the fireplace and leans on the mantle. Maybe he didn't realize how close the killer was to him. Someone right in his neighborhood did this to his friends. I walk over to him and put my hand on his back. He jumps when I touch him.

"Are you okay?" I ask this time.

He doesn't respond.

"We need to go to the police. We know what's happened." I urge him. "We've got to do something." He walks away from me again, this time to the aquarium that's glowing in the corner of his living room. Terrell lets out a deep sigh. I can tell he is hurt. He looks at me like he wants to say something, but nothing comes out.

"Let's ask your mother to take us to the police right now. We have to tell Maria and Dorothy." I envision both their faces and the heavy sobs they've succumbed to these past few days.

"Mr. Norton wasn't out that time of night," he says plainly.

"Yes, he was. He did it."

"No, he didn't," he says a little sharper. His eyes are on me, but they do not make me feel comfortable as I've once felt from looking at them. "He was not out there at all that night," he says again.

"But you don't know that."

"Yes, I do," he says with conviction.

"But you told me that you were nowhere around when it happened." He looks at me and then down at the floor. I stand to my feet. "How do you know?" I say louder. "Were you out there?"

"Yes."

"Did you see what happened?"

He looks away from me. I get closer to him and ask him the same question through gritted teeth.

"I know what happened." A tear falls down his cheek. He turns his back to me and says he doesn't want to talk about it.

"Please tell me. I need to know," I beg. He faces me.

The sun no longer shines into the window likes it's done before, brightening his eyes. His eyes are darker, his facial muscles tightened. I can see the bone move in and out from his jawline, gritting his teeth. I've never seen him look like this. It scares me.

"They hurt Nicole." That's how he starts. My stomach twists in knots when he says it. I know what's coming next. I can see it in his eyes. The words sit on the tip of his tongue like a violent predator.

"What do you mean they hurt Nicole? And who is *they*?"

"Jason and Bobby. They hurt her." He shakes as he speaks. "Nicole liked Bobby, but she didn't know I knew. He convinced her to come to Jason's when Jason's parents were out of town and they raped her." He plops on the couch and puts his head into his hands. He rubs his head as if he is trying to brush the memory away. He sobs. I can't see his face, but I hear the sniffles.

"That night she came into the house I had just gotten out the bed to get a glass of water. I could tell she was shocked to see me. More than that, I could tell she was scared. I asked her where'd she been, but she didn't answer. She ran to her room and I didn't say anything else to her, not until a few days later. She was acting weird, didn't want to come out her bedroom and didn't want to go outside and walk down the street like she used to." He wipes a tear away from his face as he speaks. I stand listening, scared of the way this conversation is going. "And then one night when Momma wasn't home, I talked to her. I pretty much made her tell me what happened with her, why was she acting so weird. And she told me they'd raped her in Jason's living room."

I shake my head not believing this story.

"I knew I had to do something," he said.

He sounds unreal when he says it. It seems like it is a nasty rumor that has spread through fifty mouths and now has reached me. I turn away from him. I don't want to believe it because I knew Bobby.

"Bobby wouldn't do anything like this."

"You try telling my sister that," he says sharply.

"So, what happened? Did you...?" I don't want to say it. I don't want to believe that the person I've finally decided to trust, the person that I have judged to be a good person is really a killer.

He looks wildly at me, "What would you have done if you were me? Tell me that." He pauses and turns his back to me.

My entire body trembles. My knees feel like Jell-O. I look him directly in the eyes and ask him the question that I don't want to assume the answer to. "Did you kill Bobby?"

He doesn't answer. I back away from him, stumbling toward the front door. He continues to move closer, but his hand is stretched toward me. *Is he going to hurt me?* I trip over the side table and fall onto the floor. Then I hear a voice. It's Sharon. "Terrell," she yells downstairs. He looks upward and I stumble to my feet. "Terrell, is everything okay?" I open the door quickly and run across the yard, making my way to Dorothy's house without looking back.

All I know is I've got to get away from Beautiful Lane, there is nothing beautiful about this place.

Dorothy meets me as soon as I come into the house, but I rush past her and go directly into the bathroom. I lean against the bathroom door and take my shirt to wipe the tears from my face.

She knocks on the door and asks where I'd been and if everything is okay.

No, nothing is okay.

Then there's another person talking to her. The voice sounds familiar and I realize it is Anthony. All I wanted to do was get away from Terrell and now I need to get away from this neighborhood.

"I'll be out in a minute," I finally say after inhaling my asthma pump. When I open the door, she leans against the wall waiting for me. Her eyes look worried and she grabs my hand and asks me what is going on. Anthony is no longer in the hall with her.

"It's the Nortons," I whisper.

"What about them? Are they okay?" She looks toward the window as if she can see into their home.

"Mr. Norton attacked me last night."

"He did what?" She says louder.

I put a finger to my lips so she will be a little quieter.

"We have to call the police," she suggests.

"No please don't. Terrell was there and he helped me. He hit Mr. Norton with an object, and he could get into trouble too. Please don't tell Sharon or anyone else what happened." The only reason I don't want her to say anything is not because of the Nortons, but in some sense I know Terrell will be exposed for what he's done, and I don't know if I am ready for that to happen.

Dorothy looks at me sadly and gives me a consoling hug.

"Okay, I won't say anything. I'm thankful you are okay though."

AFTER I FINISH cleaning myself up, I come downstairs and there's Anthony sitting to the breakfast nook drinking from a mug. He sips it slowly. Dorothy is quiet. She moves around the kitchen like everything is okay, like everything is back to normal because Anthony has returned. She hums a familiar tune as she sweeps the crumbs from the floor that she's wiped from the countertop. As I watch her, I feel like I have betrayed them. I know who their son's murderer is; yet, I am protecting him. I am keeping it hidden in a safe place, never to be discussed with anyone else. Maybe I am the only one who knows. Maybe Nicole knows too.

"I'm leaving tomorrow," I say abruptly. Dorothy stops sweeping and Anthony takes the mug away from his lips.

"Where are you going to go?" Dorothy asks.

"I haven't figured it out yet. I need to look into something tonight and then I'll know for sure. Dorothy puts the broom down and comes to hug me. I don't know how, but I think I've filled the void in her life. Anthony looks at me and smiles. She stands arm length away and only looks at me. "You will be fine," she says as she pats both of my shoulders at the same time, then readjusting my shirt.

"Excuse me. I need to go upstairs." They both nod as I leave the table. I go upstairs only to cry. I know things will get better for me. I know one day I will have a mom in my life that will love me and care for me. Maybe I have brothers who will kill for me too. I think of all the people I've lived with. I refuse to go back to Darla's place. I can't go back to the Wesley's and anyone before that has probably forgotten all about me. My reflection bounces back to me as I stand in the mirror. Idaho and its jagged edges glare back. I've learned there are things far more hideous than the mark on my face. There are other things in life I must face besides this scar. I look at Terrell's house. A figure approaches a window on the second floor. It's Sharon, looking out her window as well. For a moment I hope to see Terrell.

My bag is in the corner, leaning against the wall. I pick it up and put my little bit of things back into it, including the things Dorothy gave me. One by one, I fold them as tears roll down my cheek. I never thought the moment would come where I'd find Bobby's killer and do nothing about it. I am disappointed with myself. In some weird sense I feel like I am protecting Bobby too. Why would a star athlete, with loving parents, do something so heinous? I zip the bag firmly, toss it to the floor, and fall on the bed, crying into the pillow.

Angel
April 14, 2014
Morning

I change my mind about not telling her the truth. I finish writing the note before there's a knock at the bedroom door. I figure I can still help in all this since Terrell, Nicole, and Sharon are leaving. I've seen a moving truck to their house earlier, but I wouldn't dare ask any questions. Dorothy has the right to know and I owe it to Bobby. He became the brother I never had, and I can't forget that he's saved my life. I fold it neatly and place it on the pillow.

"Coming out shortly."

We get into the car after Dorothy hugs and kisses me and wishes me well. Anthony agrees to take me to the bus stop. I ask him to stop at Maria's driveway before we leave Beautiful Lane. He does. I walk to her front door and ring the melodious doorbell. She opens the door and smiles at me. Without saying a word, I give her a big hug. Her hair smells sweet. I want to tell her who killed her son, that it wasn't her husband's fault.

"Where's Daniel?" These are the only words I manage to say.

"He's packed his things and he's gone," she says. I nod my head, but don't comment. He deserves to be gone. He cheated with her friend and wasn't there to support her.

All I did was come to Beautiful Lane to pay respects to my friend. Things aren't as they appear to be. The people around me seemed normal until I was able to get up close and personal. They are no different than Darla and her family, disastrous; duplicitous.

Maria grabs my hand as I turn away and mouths "thank you." I didn't do anything but try to uncover the truth. I get back into the car and Anthony looks stoic.

"So, you've become friends with her since you've been here?"

"I wouldn't call it friends. Just associates."

He releases a stifled chuckle. As we drive towards the stop sign, I look in the rearview mirror and I see him. Mr. Norton has emerged from his house since the incident. He takes off in a light jog when we pull away.

"Have you decided where you are going?" He asks. As a matter of fact, I have. I want to find her. I want to know who she is. I want to know my history and how my life has turned out this way.

"I'm going west." The money that's accumulated in my account will suffice for a couple of months.

"Oh really! What's out there?" He's talking to me now more than he has since I arrived on April 3rd. He seems less stressful at times, but then other times he seems tense. He is hard to read.

"My mother is out there," I say persuasively. I believe I will find her. I know I will. He gives an agreeing nod in my direction. We turn down another road and it is then I see Dell Park.

It is much busier than the time I've come here. The conversation that I had with the man crosses my mind. I remember the money and how all that information seemed so important just a few weeks ago. I look at Anthony to see if there are permanent scars on his face, but there's nothing, just a smooth beard covering a square chin, connecting to his sideburns.

"I'm going to miss you and Dorothy," I say.

"I'm sure Dorothy enjoyed your company."

We drive past a small corner store and I see something that I never thought I'd see again. It is Darla's car. Dan sits on the passenger side, fully alert and paying attention to every turn. I face forward, hoping they don't see me. They turn right, as we go straight. Anthony continues to drive and a horn blows violently behind us. My heart pounds. I think Darla and Dan must've seen me. Anthony glances in the rearview mirror and so do I. It is a silver car trailing us closely, not Darla's car. When Anthony speeds up, the other car speeds as well, blowing the horn violently and swerving from side to side. Finally, the car whips wildly down another street and is out of our sight.

"That was crazy," I say. He doesn't respond. He looks nervous. "Are you okay?"

"Yeah...yeah I'm good." He glares out the rearview window again. "So how long are you going to be out west?" He doesn't ask the question as if he really cares. It's obvious he wants to get my attention off what just happened.

"I'm unsure. For as long as it takes for me to find her." He's not listening. He seems agitated by something. We pull to the bus stop and sit there for a moment.

"Are you sure you're okay?" I was feeling better about him since I discovered the truth about Terrell, but now something doesn't seem quite right about Anthony. He's sweating. His eyes are searching the area we are in. I reach for my bags on the back seat and get out the car. He gives me an awkward smile again and waves to me as I walk on the bus. I imagine Dorothy at home waiting for him to return, smiling as he walks through the door. I wish she was here to wave me off to a new start.

I think about the people on Beautiful Lane, all the secrets they have kept inside for so long, secrets that have destroyed the lives they were used to. Finding my seat, I lean my head against the window, watching Anthony back out the parking lot. Suddenly, he slams on breaks. A car darts out in front of him. Low chatter fills the bus as the engine revs for me to head west. I imagine her face and I picture it being smooth and gorgeous. Her hair just as long as mine used to be. The bus pulls forward as I see another car pull behind Anthony. It is the same car that honked its horn wildly behind us just moments ago. My eyes widen. A man gets out the car quickly. I want to yell *stop,* but I can't. I want to yell *No, please don't,* but the words are choked. A gun is raised and then the faint sound of a pop. The bus pulls away from the station as I look on in disbelief. The first car pulls away quickly, and so does the other one.

I slouch in my seat covering my face -disbelief written on it- as I head west to find my mother.

Epilogue
Dorothy
April 14, 2014

Angel is gone. I will miss her. She filled a special place in my heart since Bobby is no longer here. I would never try to replace him, but with all the things that have been going on, it was good to have another person in the house with me since Anthony was always in and out taking care of business. Anthony offered to take her to the bus station. He said he had to stop a couple of places anyway, so it wasn't a problem to drop her off. I kissed her on the cheek before she left. I didn't plan to do it, but it was as if she'd become my own child within these last two weeks.

When she told me what happened the other night at the Norton's, I knew it was a lie. She probably wants attention or usually struggles and competes for attention between siblings in foster homes. I explained it to Anthony and asked we not hold it against her. "She is trying to figure out who she is and how to fit in. She's never had a real family," I said. "It can't be true. Who wouldn't want something like that reported? And they are such sweet people."

I go to the guest room to see if there is anything that needs to be cleaned. The room is just as clean and fresh as it was before she came. She was a good guest. The pictures on the nightstand sit firmly in place. The curtains rest against the window, still. The quilt is smoothed out neatly across the bed. The pillows are fluffed. There's something on the pillow, a piece of paper. I pick it up and it has on the top, For Dorothy. I sit on the bed to open the letter, looking over the outside of it first. I look at the ceiling, imagining her telling me how thankful she is that I let her stay here with us. I fumble to open the letter, but the doorbell rings, the Christmas tune that we haven't changed. I look outside, but there's no car. *Maybe they're parked on the other side of the house.*

I rush downstairs, unlatch the door, and two people stand here, a short, chubby lady with red hair and a rough looking guy. He removes his shades and asks, "Is Angel here?" My eyes scan his tattooed arms. His green eyes aren't as attractive as others I've seen. His are somber, dark.

I'm a little shocked at first. These people do not look like anyone Angel would know.

"I'm sorry, she's not here."

"Are you sure? See, we're her foster parents and she ran away from home," the woman says. Her red lipstick doesn't suit her well and a dab rests on her two front teeth. I am not sure how to respond to her so I only answer the previous way I have.

"I'm sorry, she's not here."

Suddenly the guy lunges forward, forcing himself into my house. I let out a scream that pierce my own ears. I run through the foyer and into the dining room. He yells, "Angel, where are you?"

I run through the kitchen and into the downstairs bathroom. I hear his boots clogging against the floor. He approaches the door I've just closed and bangs against it with anger.

"Please leave me alone. She is not here." What have I gotten myself into by allowing her to come to my house and how do these people know where I live?

He rams his shoulder into the door two times and then stops abruptly. He stomps away and things fall in my house, pictures clattering to the floor. I imagine Bobby's picture falling, frame shattered, just as our life has shattered when he'd fallen to the ground that night. I curl in the bathroom floor, praying they will see she is not here and will leave.

"Angel we know you're here," the woman says. She had me fooled at the door. If the guy wasn't with her, I would have given this woman all the information she needed concerning Angel. They walk upstairs. His boot slams against each door, releasing a cracking sound, forcing himself into each area of my house.

They rush back downstairs and come in front of the bathroom door again. *Why didn't I run while they were upstairs?* My body is frozen. My legs and arms will not move as if lead is keeping them down. All I can do is hold my legs to my chest, hoping Anthony is almost home.

Someone knocks on my front door again. This time it is louder. A male voice yells out, "Ms. Dorothy are you home? We're coming in." The man and woman who were once standing at my bathroom door runs down the hall.

"Hey! Hey! Stop right there! Freeze!" It is a police officer. My heart is relieved. Maybe one of my neighbors saw or heard something happening. Someone runs past the bathroom door, then another. "Stop right there." A gunshot is fired. I grip my ears in fear. Who shot at who? Is someone dead? Why is this happening?

"Ms. Dorothy, where are you?" I can tell it is a cop yelling my name. He sounds firm and helpful. I run to open the bathroom door and a tall guy stands to the door with his gun in his hand. He grabs me by my hand and takes me into the living room. I glance out the window. I see the woman in handcuffs and a thick red stain saturates the man's shirt. He is on the ground in handcuffs too.

"Are you okay, Ma'am?" Tears stream down my face.

"No, I'm not okay. I'm just so thankful that someone called you. I couldn't get to a phone or anything." The officer sits beside me and gives me a compassionate look.

He touches my hand and says, "No one called us here. We've come here for a different reason."

I stop and just stare at him. *Did you find my son's killer? Do you know who did this to my son?*

He clears his throat and looks me in my eyes. "Ma'am, your husband was just shot at a nearby bus station."

My heart is ripped from my chest. The news is too unbearable. I look at him and ask the hardest question I could ever ask. "Is he dead?"

"Ma'am, I think you should get to the hospital as soon as possible."

I rush to my car, letter still gripped between my fingers, to go to the hospital. The cops put the woman in the patrol car. The EMT's put the man on the ambulance. I back out the yard and head to the hospital, not knowing if Anthony is dead or alive.

Nicole
April 13, 2014
Afternoon

Mom says we are moving, and I am glad. I just want to start over, allow me and Terrell another chance at a real life without the problem of my mistake hanging over my head. All my things are packed and so is Terrell's. He stands to my bedroom door for a short moment and it's almost as if I know what he is thinking. *I love you, sis.* I grab my diary from my drawer, hoping no one else will ever read it. I don't even know if I want Mama knowing the truth about this incident. She would feel even more horrible for neglecting us.

I pick up one bag remaining in the floor, tuck my journal into it and walk downstairs to meet Mama and Terrell. The movers have loaded everything, but I decide to leave my drawer and Bobby's picture hidden inside. Mama closes the door behind her, leaving me and Terrell's secret locked inside and hidden in the cracks of Beautiful Lane. We get into the car and drive out the driveway. I look at Jason's house one last time. I notice Terrell does the same thing. I see myself on that evil night and wish I could take it back, rearrange the events from that night, making it a lovely masterpiece. My eyes water, but I hold back the tears and we head towards our new home.

Daniel
April 14, 2014
Morning

I pick up the phone to call Maria. It goes straight to voicemail. I put down the phone trying to figure out what to do to get my wife back. I can't believe I was so stupid. I shouldn't have put my feelings before hers. I shouldn't have cheated at all. I was grateful when she'd taken me back the first time after my infidelities, but then I broke her heart again during the most challenging time of our lives.

I grab my keys and phone. I dial her number once more and again, no answer. I get into the car, knowing I've got to see her. I must talk to her face to face. There is no way to get her to understand what I've done, but I must ask for forgiveness. If she doesn't take me back, then I'll have to accept it. I drive through downtown and past Anthony. It looks like that girl is in the car, but I pay little attention to trying to figure it all out.

As I turn onto Beautiful Lane, my heart begins to leap, not from joy, but from nervousness. I don't know what I will say to her. She does not want to see me. I pull into our driveway and wait patiently. I want to run in, just kiss her and apologize, but I know that won't fix this big mess I've made. I turn the ignition switch off and remain in the car for a few minutes. Another car pulls onto Beautiful Lane, but parks at the end of the street. It is a chubby woman with a taller guy. I pay little attention to who they are, but before I get out the car, I see them walk to Dorothy's house. I walk to my side door, stick my key in and it still works. I walk into my house after glancing at Dorothy's once more and I see her standing talking to the man and woman. I close my door and place my keys on the table.

The house is quiet. There's no television, no movement. I peek into the living room and there's no Maria. Our bedroom is empty, only the fresh scent of her shampoo lingers. I miss that smell. I walk further down the hall and push Jason's bedroom door open. Maria sits on a neatly fixed bed, gazing out our son's window. I push open the door and it doesn't startle her. She only gazes at me as if she expected me.

"I'm sorry," are the only words I can utter.

She shakes her head and a tear rolls down her face. I sit beside her, and she allows me to hold her hand.

"I am so sorry, Maria. I shouldn't have cheated on you."

She stands to her feet and walks to the window. She looks out toward the pond behind our house. "You've told me that before," she says calmly. "How could you do this to me again?"

I stand behind her. "I am so stupid. I didn't want to deal with the pain of losing Jason."

"And what about the policy?" She asks quickly.

"I should've talked to you about it, but he lived a reckless life. I didn't know what else to do. I couldn't stop him, and I know this may sound horrible, but I knew there was only a matter of time."

Maria let out a whimper. I put my arms around her shoulders. I should've been here with her to ease her pain. I should've have helped her. I've failed as a father, but I don't have to fail as a husband.

"Please let me come back. I will never hurt you again."

"I just don't know," she said. "I have learned to pray during this difficult. When I thought prayer wouldn't work, I have found it gives me peace."

Suddenly, there is an influx of sirens screaming in our neighborhood. I cannot imagine what has happened. Maria and I go to the front door and cops are at Dorothy's house. We watch from the front step. The cops go into the house and we hear shots fired. The man and woman are brought out by an officer and are on the ground. A few short minutes later, Dorothy comes out the house and rushes to her car. Maria wants to run over and so do I, but Dorothy is already pulling out the yard. Maria slides her fingers between mine. I know she wants me to make her feel safe. I know she wants us to be better than who we are. She deserves better. She shouldn't worry about pain coming from outside and inside her home. I kiss her forehead and we walk back into our semi-peaceful home.

ACKNOWLEDGMENTS

I thank God for giving me the mind to function in my creative abilities that He has so graciously blessed me with and for giving me the strength to finish what I started. I am proud to have an imagination that will cause fictitious situations to seem real.

I am deeply thankful for my mother for being the listening ear as I learned more about my characters and needed to talk about them. When I decided to change the title from *Beautiful Secrets* to something else, she gave me the title *The Secrets They Kept.* Thanks Mommy.

Thank you to Tracy Hart, who asked me one question after reading my first draft and it changed the trajectory of this book. Thanks for having an editor's eye.

Thanks to my students: Erica Garcia, Michelle Vainqueur and Tahlya Edgerton, from my first block English 9 class, who willingly read their favorite teacher's book with enthusiasm when it was in its third draft. I am very appreciative of you girls. As I believed in my students' dreams, they believed in mine. DREAM BIG!

Thanks to Jimeka Joynes, Shaleeta Radford, Cynthia Haynes, Yovanda Brown, Chester Hall and Keith Moody for jumping on board without hesitation. I am appreciative of you. Thank you to all my community readers who started and finished reading the book before it was published. Your participation means a lot to me and my heart leaps when I think of the much support I received from you all. Thanks to Maurice Banister for being patient with my writing on windows with expo markers, sticky notes on walls, and answering my questions on the topic of "what would a father do if..."

This task was so important to me and you all stepped up to the plate to assist in fulfilling my dream. It means more to me than you will ever know. I hope you all are prepared for the next books to come.

This has been a wonderful, contemplative, unsure, exciting journey. I look forward to doing it again.

ABOUT THE AUTHOR

Photo by Erin Sharrow

Lakishia Banister studied English Literature at Salisbury University and holds a Master of Arts in Teaching from the University of Maryland Eastern Shore. She is the author of the inspirational self-help book, *Overcome the Obstacle: Pursue the Dream.* Lakishia is the mother of three and an educator. She resides in Williamsburg, VA.

Website: lakishiabanister.org
Facebook: LakishiaBanister
Instagram: @lakishiabanister
Twitter: @lakishiab
Email: lakishiabanister@gmail.com

Lakishia Banister

Reading Group Guide

The Secrets They Kept

A Novel

Lakishia Banister

Questions and topics
for discussion and book clubs

1. When Angel is on the bus heading to Northern Virginia, she looks at a young lady who has gotten off the bus and realize her thoughts about her were wrong. Angel then says, "That's what I do. I think something about someone only to find out I was wrong." How does this statement foreshadow upcoming events in the plot?

2. After Angel arrives to Dorothy's house, she is asked a question, but she doesn't want to lie. She believes it is too much work. On the contrary, Angel lies quite often throughout the novel. Do you believe she is a legitimate liar or has lying become a necessity? Explain.

3. The first time Angel sees Maria's house she describes the beauty of the outside. When she visits Maria, she notices minor things in the kitchen such as dishes needing to be washed. But when Angel sees Maria's closet it appears to be a big mess. She makes the statement that, "clothes hang on for dear life." Later, clothes are out of closets and in the living room and hallway, creating a bigger mess. Interpret your perception of Maria's life based on Angel's view from beauty on the outside of the house to mess and clutter deeper within the house.

4. How does Dorothy's cleanliness in hidden areas reflect her life?

5. Jason has a pair of red, white, and blue sneakers and a pair of muddy boots by the door. How do these shoes represent different moments of Jason's life?

6. There are so many clues around Maria pertaining to Jason: the blue polo shirt, fingernail file, black boots, squeaking floor, broken picture frame and more. But these items are nothing to really pay attention to. As parents, do you think daily clues are constantly around us about the teenagers in our lives? Give examples.

7. Jason seems disconnected from his father, Daniel, unlike Bobby who seems to be close to his father. After Jason sees his father with another woman, he asks Bobby, "Wouldn't you know your dad if you saw him? It wouldn't matter what covered his face or what was going on. You would know your dad." Bobby understands what Jason means at this moment. What is the irony of this dialogue?

8. Throughout the novel characters either look at themselves in the <u>mirror</u> as they reflect or gaze out the <u>window</u>. Interpret the symbolism of each item.

9. Why do you think Jason felt raping Nicole would've been revenge against Sharon?

10. Who do you blame for Bobby and Jason's death? Terrell, Nicole, Daniel, Sharon, or their own actions? Explain.

11. Anthony borrows money from a king pin and eventually kills him. What does this say about Anthony's character?

12. Do you believe Anthony's behavior reflects his old neighborhood? How?

13. Mrs. Norton's backstory involves her father being murdered in front of her while he was at the playground with her. She was only seven. He was pushing her on the swing when some guys robbed and shot him. How do you think this past incident affects Mrs. Norton's current behavior?

14. When Angel arrives to Beautiful Lane she says, "the grass is really greener on the other side." What does this say about how we look at things on the surface in other people's lives?

15. When Angel sees Nicole, she says she tries to fit her personal story on Nicole, but it fits her like a "too big, flimsy outfit." She also mentions earlier in the novel that she is often wrong about what she thinks of people. How do these statements coincide when comparing Nicole and Angel's life?

16. Compare and Contrast Bobby's old neighborhood and Beautiful Lane.

17. At one point or another in the novel characters begin to wonder what their neighbors will think of them if they discover their secrets. Do you think this concern is due to the respect they have for one another or is it about image?

18. The reality of people's lives can be drastically different from the way we view them. How do the people on Beautiful Lane view one another? How is this like our own society and the way we look at others?

19. Do you believe Anthony's reason was justified for murdering the king pin? Did he deserve to die? Why?

20. Although many youth are flourishing and prospering in the world, many people believe this is the most troubled generation. How does Angel, Bobby, Jason, Terrell, and Nicole each represent our millennial generation?

Lakishia Banister

Made in the USA
Middletown, DE
21 December 2021